THE GOD OF ALL GOOD THINGS

THE GODDESS OF ORIGIN
BOOK TWO

CHIARA FORESTIERI

For those who feel like they 'just can't' anymore... Try to remember to keep yourself receptive to the divinely orchestrated chaos of the universe. You are loved.

"Everyone follows my path, knowingly or unknowingly. All paths, ultimately, lead to me..."
- The Bhagavad Gita

GLOSSARY

Aurelia (Or-el-lia) Goddess of Origin and Guardian of Souls - Power to draw souls in or out of their body. Nexus Mate to Kyril.

Kyril (Kye-ril) Half vampire/Half Fae (or so we assumed) - Power to burn someone from the inside out and reduce them to ashes. Nexus Mate to Aurelia.

Quetzalcoatl (Ketz-Uh-Ko-At-L) | A.K.A Quetz (Ketz)- The Winged Serpent God, The God of All Good Things, The Winds and Rain, The Arts, and Time. A.K.A The Lonely Creator God of Time and Benevolence. Alternative form: The Winged Serpent. Originally from another dimension, he traversed the realms and time as he was drawn to Aeternia to eventually allow himself to be trapped by Kyril in an enchanted mirror to spend 33 years in Queen's Nuala's dungeons waiting for Aurelia to arrive so that he could plant the seed that would eventually blossom into The Creators' Promise binding them...

Queen Nuala (Noo-lah) - Queen of the Aeternian Realm - Most powerful known Fae on Aeternia. Alternative form: Chimera. Best friend to Aurelia and Kyril. Casual lover of Quetz. Nexus Mate: unknown.

Batlaan (Baht-lahn) - Lord of the Eastern Guard and mate to Eleni. Son of Morwen. Nexus mate to Eleni.

Eleni (Eh-Lay-Nee) - Daughter of the late Emperor Lussathir to the Lux Dryadalin Realm who previously trapped her on the Caligoan realm for 20 years before her nexus mate, Batlaan, could free her.

Morwen (More-when) - The most powerful known shamaness and sorceress on Aeternia. Mother to Batlaan. Nexus Mate to Nox.

Nox (Noks) Prince of the Tenebris Drydalis realm. Nexus Mate to Morwen.

Lisbet (Liz-bet)(see 'Mute') - A powerful entity who came from a realm beyond *the nine*. A mute. Nexus Mate to Idra.

Idra (Eed-rah) the ever silent and ever observant *draconi*/dragon shifter,

Aelia (Ale-leah) - The newly widowed and former Empress and Oracle to the Lux Dryadalis realm. Spent 90 years quarantined from the rest of the realms in the west wing of the palace (forced by her late husband, Lussathir). Lussathir then murdered her in order to use her body as a vessel for the spirit of his deceased Nexus Mate. Her daughter in-law persuaded Aurelia to bring Aelia's spirit back to her body before her father could bring back his mate. Her own Nexus Mate is yet to be discovered.

Nahui (Nah—whee) - Magical serpent who is bound to Quetz. Is an ancestor of Ouroboros.

Caelus (Kay-luss) - God of the Lightning, the Skies, Humanity, and Justice. Uncle to Kyril Ronan.

Ahualei (Ah-wah-lay) - Goddess of Water, Fertility, Motherhood, the Ometäian Realm's Underworld.

Mute - A being from another dimension stuck in an incorporeal form, forced to wander the realms without access to the five physical senses, and is thusly driven to steal a corporeal form by killing someone, unless they just happen to be nearby when someone die.

INTRODUCTION

I hope that... whoever you are, wherever you are, reading this book brings you joy, and nourishes your soul in some capacity (no matter how small), and that you can feel all the love I put into it. And perhaps if so, that love will plant a tiny seed- or perhaps be the sun and water to a seed that simply needed some nourishment- within you so that it can blossom and grow into something so wonderful in your life, that it can't help but bear a loving fruit to others.

Writing this book has been one of the most fulfilling and unexpected experiences of my life. For the last week (today is January 10th, 2023), I didn't leave my house once and instead bunkered down in my hide-y hole to write it.

I cannot claim that anything or anyone other some unseen muse poured the beauty of their soul into mine and I was merely the conduit in putting pen to paper. Or pressing finger to key, rather (thank you muse and thank you fingers). And some of you may think it's complete and utter shit, for which I am sorry, but I'll just have to be ok with that. Different strokes for different folks. I still love you and kindly ask that you *please* be kind and take into consideration that, like all artists- authors among them- the words written in a book are a fragment of a reflection of someone's soul. And it takes courage to reveal such a thing to anyone, much less the general public.

That being said, I do not, for one second, take your precious time and energy for granted. We are all so busy and often profoundly over-whelmed, and absorbed by the chaos of the world. She is a seemingly mercurial mistress... Though I do suspect that ultimately she just wants us to grow together and ascend to something beautiful and joyous and wonderful. Like love.

So thank you.

I love you for all that your beautiful soul is, in all its nigh-infinite potential and glory. I genuinely wish you the best.

- Chiara

PLEASE NOTE

In the first book of this series, there were numerous wildly explicit love/sex scenes that came on rather quickly between Aurelia and her nexus mate, Kyril. And their whirlwind romance took up more of the center stage as the book progressed.

This book, however, while still intense, the romance is much more of a slow burn. But there is one particularly long, explicit and highly graphic love/sex scene. It's takes up all of Chapter 19 (one page), and Chapter 20. So if that's not your thing then... Well, perhaps skimming through it would be better if it's too much for you.

ONE

AURELIA

E leni's eyes filled with tears and spilt down her cheeks. Quetz stepped forward and took up the spot beside Aelia whose gaze seemed to pass through Eleni as she spoke distantly. "Quetzacoatl, The Lonesome Creator God of Time and Benevelonce... I do wonder where your destiny lies...."

Quetzacoatl's mouth quirked upwards in one corner as he studied her, his luminous eyes dimming slightly at her words.

"I stopped asking myself that question worlds ago..."

He heaved a sigh. "Will you help us find the one looking for the sigillums? And then Aurelia can send you back home?"

Aelia's gaze finally rose to meet Quetz. Before it slid and settled on Kyril like a boulder.

The group of us seemed to hold our breath. Even Kyril seemed uncertain in the moment. Surely, the weight of Aelia's pointed, silvery gaze implied something else... My heart hammered with panic desperate for it to mean, literally, anything else, other than that it had been Kyril seeking the seven sigillums that could open the doorway between dimensions. And, most likely, destroy our world.

Aelia gave him a sad smile as she finally spoke. "The things we do to avoid suffering often become the very cause of it..."

Nuala stood beside me and slipped a steadying hand over my shoulder. I could feel the pain and anger radiating from her at Aelia's implication. "Speak plainly, oracle."

Aelia's gaze didn't budge from Kyril's as she spoke, wholly unaffected by Nuala's terse tone. "Perhaps, your hybrid god," the group of us gasping and breath catching at the words, "would like to explain himself but... I am... too tired. Now that my husband is gone and *you*," she added bitterly as her gaze slammed into me, "Have again confined me to this gods-forsaken *shell*... I am going to liberate myself of this glorified cage called a palace... And Eleni, I know it's not what you wanted but the future of the realm must lie in your hands. Do with it what you will." Aelia rose and strode out of the room, leaving us all gaping in silence.

Eleni chased after her. Batlaan looked between us all- flashing Kyril a look, stricken with hurt and disappointment, before following Eleni out of the room. His words were soft and bitter, but far less angry than I'd have expected of him.

"This is not over, brother."

Kyril's expression darkened, an undercurrent of sadness permeating it, before he managed to steel himself. His eyes softened when his gaze returned to mine. My voice shook with my swelling emotions: a whorling melange of fury, fear, disappointment, and sadness.

"How? Why?... Why would you do this?"

Kyril spoke with shocking calm and remorselessness as he shifted towards me. I didn't have the good sense to step away from him. He was my nexus mate. My eyes swelled with tears as he drew his hands up to gently cradle my face. His dark amber gaze burning into mine as he looked down at me and spoke for all to hear.

"Because even you, my beloved goddess, cannot control the future. You were taken from me once- and I'm merely ensuring that it never happens again... I will not be stopped. Even by you, my fire."

Opening that gateway would mean the potential destruction of our realm. At the very least, death to thousands, if not millions, of Aeternians. And only gods knew what type of entities would try to conquer it. The war and bloodshed that would ensue was unfathomable.

Kyril had spent over 200 years mourning my death until I had been reincarnated 33 years ago... though he had eventually taken other lovers during this time. Something for which I was grateful. I couldn't even begin to imagine the suffering Kyril had endured, having his nexus mate murdered, and finding my formerly *decapitated* body with its heart having been carved out... *By his own Uncle.* A detail that I had yet to find a free moment to bring up since I'd discovered this truth.

Regardless, it went without saying that opening that gateway was far too high a price to pay to ensure we'd never be separated again. In this life, or the next. Tears slipped over the dams of my eyelids and he kissed them away.

"Bringing certain suffering to others to spare your own is not the answer," I croaked out softly.

A coldness I'd never seen before entered his gaze that normally smouldered like the embers of a fire.

"If I have to become a monster to protect you, Aurelia, so be it."

I shook my head in disbelief.

"Solely to spare yourself the pain of my absence is unfathomably selfish."

His brows slammed down.

"Selfish? Think of all the suffering that would end. Mates reunited. Families made whole again. How could you say that?"

"You're not one of The Creators, Kyril."

His expression only hardened.

"I'll be whoever I need to be to protect you and keep you with me."

"Protect me? Lussathir just kidnapped me, put a palladium collar on my neck, and very nearly succeeded in killing me! All because of you!"

"He was unhinged. It's what happens when you lose your nexus mate," he retorted remorselessly, "And if I had known he had planned such a thing, I would have killed him myself. But it just further proves my point. Why we need to open that fucking doorway. None of this would have happened if it was. Imagine the suffering that could be prevented! Isn't that worth fighting another war for if it prevents so much suffering?"

My heart shattered a little more, what was left of it, witnessing what had become of my nexus in the time I'd been gone. My words came out little more than a whisper.

"What have you become?"

Before he could respond, Morwen stepped forward, her sharp features pulled tight, blood splatter decorating her face and her clothes. Nox stood beside her in solidarity.

"Kyril... I thought you, of all people, would understand the consequences of upsetting the balance and barriers between realms..."

Kyril leaned down briefly to sweep a kiss over my forehead before his hands left my face as he straightened to face Morwen and Nox.

"And yet, even with these barriers war, violence, and the insatiable thirst for power remain. Perhaps it is time to try an alternative. Perhaps uniting the unknown realms will bring peace."

Morwen's face hardened.

"You are using wishful thinking to pacify your guilt, Kyril. It will not work. And I will not allow you to try."

A corner of Kyril's mouth slowly curved upwards. His velvety, baritone voice took on a foreboding calm.

"You would try to stop me?"

Nox took a step beyond Morwen towards Kyril as if to both shield her and speak for both of them.

"Just as you would to protect your mate, I will protect mine. "

Idra joined them followed by his mate Lisbet.

Nuala still stood behind me, facing Kyril. She did nothing to mask the anguish in her voice.

"We worked so hard to bring peace to this realm. Aurelia *died* for it. And now you not only wish to throw it all way, you betrayed us. This whole time we were chasing the sigillums- risking our lives- because of *you*. You were working with *Lussathir* for gods-sake."

Kyril's mask of indifference faltered briefly.

"Betraying your trust pained me greatly... But was I wrong to assume that you would have joined me if I had been honest? And it wasn't for nothing. I'm sure you'll agree that Yiruxat was long over due her expiration. We saved hundreds of slaves. We reunited Idra and Lisbet."

The silent tension in the room grew.

Kyril shook his head sadly.

"I'm sorry for all I've done to destroy your faith in me. I hope you can empathize with my justifications and one day appreciate what I'm doing. I'm fairly certain that, if something happened to any of your nexus mates... You'd all go to the same lengths."

"Where are the sigillums now?" Nox asked grimly.

I caught Nuala's eyes as Kyril spoke, cutting me off.

"With my Uncle."

I froze, jaw dropping just before Kyril pulled me into him, my chest pressing just beneath his, and wrapped his arms around me.

I tried to shove away from him but it only caused him to tighten his grip to the point of pain making me growl in protest.

"Kyril, you're hurting me. Let me the fuck *go*."

"You're coming with me, Aurelia."

"Do I not have a choice in the matter?" I spat.

Quetz stepped forward, his expression and voice darkening in a way that could only be interpreted as a threat.

"You were there when I swore my vow to protect her... Let her go."

Kyril's gaze slowly shifted to him as a grin that promised violence curled his lips.

Before he could spout any vitriol I folded out of his arms and reappeared behind him, backing slowly away as he moved again towards me.

"Can we discuss this and come up with some kind of alternative solution? Opening the sigillums would be a death wish made manifest."

Kyril slowly approached me like you would a cornered, feral animal. "We can discuss whatever you want but you will not change my mind, and I need you to come with me."

"Where? If it's to go steal the rest of the sigillums, I'm afraid I have no interest. You have to stop this. Before you do things that you can't make amends for. *Please.*"

Quetz's eyes glowed a particularly bright shade of turquoise as though illuminated from within before dimming.

Where had he just gone?

"*Quetz...*," Kyril growled knowingly, his words a warning.

Quetz's grin was borderline sadistic.

Morwen, Nox, Idra, and Lisbet took slow steps forward. As though cornering us. Black tendrils of magic began to seep from Morwen's fingers, turning the tips black.

Kyril's attention shifted to Morwen before he chuckled darkly.

"I'd *really* rather not, Morwen."

She huffed a laugh.

"I know you wouldn't. I'm sure it *pains* you to remember the last time we had a disagreement. Your nose healed beautifully though."

Kyril laughed but his words became a warning.

"*You* were the only one who resorted to violence. If I'd reciprocated, you and I both know how it would have ended..."

A low growl came from Nox's throat as ice began to slowly blossom across the floor.

Quetz's eyes met mine and gave me a subtle nod as if to reassure me before winking out of existence.

My mind reeled.

What the fuck was happening? The world's gone mad. My closest friends, my brothers and sisters in arms, my compatriots... My nexus mate... We were all suddenly pitted against the male I loved most in this world.

Despite whatever distance now laid between me and Quetz, a burst of warmth filled my chest, through The Creators' Promise that bound us.

Kyril tried to close in on me as the other's did him. He leapt to grab me, latching onto my robe just I folded to the other side of Nuala where we both landed.

Before we could crash to the ground the world around me folded into that black horizon of burning stars.

TWO

AURELIA

T he light of day shone so brightly it burned my eyes. And when I opened them Quetz was standing beside us. My heart heaved a sigh of relief. We'd arrived in...

... I wasn't entirely sure what realm we were in but we were definitely no longer in Lux Dryadalis. While the gardens we stood in were so extravagant and perfectly manicured, it was fit for a palace, the gargantuan home that lied beyond it was unlike any architecture I'd seen since... Well. Ever. Although I hadn't been to many of the realms in over two hundred years, so I imagined tastes had changed. The building was white and block-y, gold embellishing every corner and ridge, and tall white columns ensconced every overhang and footpath. Something about it seemed rather... human.

I tried to shove away from Kyril and, thankfully, he didn't object. I had never in either of my lives fathomed hurting him.

I still couldn't. But my patience was *rapidly* dwindling.

"What *the fuck* is going on with you? You just kidnapped me! Who the fuck are you?!"

Kyril completely ignored me as though I were a toddler having a temper tantrum, his focus now on Nuala, who had clutched onto me before Kyril had folded us away, and Quetz who had clearly predicted this.

"Oh for fuck's sake," Kyril growled, "What's your plan then, hm?"

Nuala scowled.

"I'm here to keep you out of trouble, even if I have to cause you grave bodily harm and restrain you, you fucking asshole. How dare you betray us like this. You're lucky I don't let my Chimera eat you alive."

Kyril took a deep breath, rubbing his brow with his thumb and forefinger.

"If by trouble you mean uniting the seals and opening the portal, I'm afraid you're going to be sorely disappointed because that's the only reason I'm here."

Nuala's and my jaw dropped in unison.

"You have all of them already?" I breathed.

Kyril's expression softened as his gaze returned to mine in apology.

"But Lisbet... She hadn't-."

"Did you really think I was going to leave it up to her after you found her?"

My jaw slackened in disbelief as a frown carved Kyril's features, staring apology at me before his shifted back to Quetz.

"You here to keep me out of trouble as well?"

"No, not really... I'm here to protect Aurelia. Although you'll need some help too, eventually... Be careful with your uncle. Bit of a temper, that one."

My stomach dropped at the mention of Kyril's Uncle, Caelus.

Quetz's gaze slammed back to mine.

Of course, he already knew. The male was nigh-omniscient thanks to his capacity to travel across space and time.

Kyril's wariness only grew. "And what of the sigillums?"

Quetz shrugged in that mindbogglingly nonchalant way of his, now picking at a particularly fascinating piece of lint on his tunic. As though the world wasn't potentially about to end.

"I'm actually not terribly concerned about them."

What did he know?

I stared in disbelief at Quetz, scrutinizing his person so thoroughly it should have drilled a hole through him. But still, it gave me no answer.

Kyril's expression grew impossibly more dour.

"It would *'actually'* be really helpful if you could enlighten us for once since you're the only one here who can access future outcomes and potentialities."

The light illuminating Quetz's eyes darkened in an instant as his gaze slammed into Kyril's.

"Careful, Kyril. There are somethings you're better off not knowing, and even more that are far beyond your control. Just as they are beyond mine."

Kyril's jaw feathered and the tension between them tightened.

Though both made no move for the other.

Thankfully, Nuala broke the tension.

"Can you at least tell us what happens if he does manage to open the doorway between realms? Then maybe our best friend, *the psychopath*, might actually be talked into reason."

Quetz shook his head. Chuckling helplessly, and looking a little crazy as he spoke in that animated and enthused way of his. "Unfortunately, no. I can't. And even worse, he won't. However, I assure you that all of them would end in the destruction of the world as we know it. But I doubt he would be able to open the sigillum's doorway anyway."

Nuala made a noise that sounded like a scoff and a growl bathed in sarcasm.

"How illuminating."

If I hadn't been so furious with Kyril at the moment I'd have laughed. And Quetz's words only made anxiety coil deeper within my gut.

"If it makes you feel any better, I'm honestly just as lost as you are most of the time. It's not like there's only a few potentialities I have to work through. Everything I see is very rarely more than potentialities. Thousands. Millions of them. And within all of those, because I'm sifting and wading through so much, I miss out on so many details. It's llike trying to sift through an ocean just to find one particular grain of sand. Not to mention, it's constantly shifting and changing. What may be a likely trajectory now, could change entirely in a matter of moments... There are, however, a great many paths that ultimately lead to the same destination. So that's reassuring. Sometimes..."

Nuala sighed heavily. "And you can't tell us about any of these particular 'destinations' either?"

Quetz hummed thoughtfully for a moment. "... No. Only that if he were to open the doorway, all of us dying is pretty much a certainty. Or perhaps indentured servitude. Total annihilation... You know... That old chestnut."

Nuala's gaze hit Kyril like a sledgehammer.

"And that doesn't worry you in the slightest?"

Kyril's gaze hardened.

"You know just as well as I do that some things are worth going to war for. Look how you became Queen."

Quetz rolled his eyes.

"You honestly have no idea what you're messing with."

Kyril's glare would have made a lesser male wither.

"While I am eternally grateful for all you've done for Aurelia, you clearly have no idea *who* you're messing with. I would implore you to not get in our way."

Quetz burst into a sudden uproarious laugh and patted a hand on Kyril's shoulder like he'd just told him some wildly clever joke.

"You're hil-larious."

Kyril's anger flashed in his expression but thankfully didn't reach the tipping point to violence. Though his response was nothing short of a growl.

"And if we return to my home, I'm guessing our friends will be waiting for us? Pitchforks in hand."

Quetz chuckled again.

"Oh, yes. If you value your friendships, I'd strongly recommend not returning until...," Quetz's eyes wandered thoughtfully over us as they flashed brightly for a moment, "Until... Well... Soon enough. You'll see."

Nuala rolled her eyes, growling at him.

"Maybe you should just stop talking for a while then. Since it's all such a big secret or all so complicated that you can't share a shred of guidance with us."

Quetz chuckled, wholly unperturbed by her jab.

Her gaze fell to the floor before returning to his, suddenly looking scalded by her own words.

"Sorry."

Quetz' smile broadened, threatening to break into a grin again. "Perhaps I should show you something that will help you better understand."

Nuala peaked a curious brow at him even as her eyes narrowed warily.

Quetz's only response was a mischievous grin and the invitation of his open palm. Nuala hesitated a moment before closing the distance between them. The moment she grasped his hand he abruptly brought his other to her forehead.

She collapsed in his arms and I gasped her name, grabbing her arm as if somehow that would steady her.

Quetz's eyes shone so brightly it almost burned *my* eyes. Like gazing into a turquoise sun.

"She'll be fine... Just needs a few moments to get her bearings. It's just *a lot* to take in."

Kyril and I exchanged a worried glance. My stomach knotting with concern as I watched Nuala's chest rise and fall with increasing speed.

A whimper left her lips.

Soon followed by a giggle.

A yelp in its wake.

She began to make a series of dramatic noises that were in such extreme contrast to one another it looked as though she were losing her mind.

My voice was far steadier than I felt.

"What're you showing her?"

"Only tiny pockets of time in her life. Putting puzzle pieces of her past together, and everything that lead to it. And also the most probable potentialities that lead to her own personal inevitable future outcomes. Nothing that will effect things negatively. Or could effect or alter the most... fortuitous... of timelines."

I took a deep breath, swallowing the knot of anxiety in my chest at watching my best friend's descent, or perhaps ascension, into madness.

Witness to her oscillating and sudden cries, laughter, groans, moans, and everything in between. Her hysteria would have even been comical if it weren't so... *real*. Instead, it was deeply unnerving.

After a few more *long* seconds, Quetz finally removed his palm from her forehead.

Tears streamed down her cheeks as her eyes blinked open. Mouth hanging slightly ajar in awe or fear or... madness, I hadn't yet discovered.

Her throat finally worked on a swallow, leaning heavily on Quetz as he carefully drew her upright. Her voice came out as a croak, tears flowing freely.

"Oh gods..."

I stepped closer to her, worry permeating my words.

"Are you ok?"

Her jaw was still slack, gobsmacked. She burst into a laugh but abruptly stopped, drawing a hand over her mouth as she began to weep gaze bouncing between us all.

Oh Gods... What had she seen?

I was now worried about *all* of us.

Quetz held her by the shoulders, grounding her. His voice gentle with care.

"Hey..."

Tears saddled her long, auburn lashes. A smile parting her beautiful lips as her gaze shifted and rose to meet his with something that I couldn't interpret to be anything less than awe.

Her voice came out a whisper.

"Thank you..."

When her gaze moved to mine her smile was almost apologetic.

My gulp was audible.

Quetz hugged her, kissing the top of her head as his gaze shifted back to me and Kyril.

Nuala chuckled, wiping tears from her face.

Kyril's expression was tight with concern and unease, flicking over Nuala who looked like she had just been put through some rollercoaster of emotion and madness.

Curiosity rose within me as to what I would find if he were to take me on such a journey but I knew now was not the time to take a journey like *that*.

Although with the way Quetz was grinning it seemed like he *definitely* had some kind of unfair advantage.

And Kyril's eyes narrowed at him as though he didn't appreciate either idea one bit.

Quetz's eyes lifted to meet Kyril's, a smirk curling one corner of his mouth.

"Perhaps *you* would like to take a peek at your own private inevitabilities, *hybrid god*."

Something like fear flashed in Kyril's eyes but before Kyril could even respond, I cut him off.

"Speaking of," I found myself growling, "'Hybrid God'? *Who* and *what* the fuck are you?"

"It's not what you think, Aurelia... I only found out after I met my Uncle. Which as you know was shortly before..."

His features hardened, Adam's apple bobbing.

"Before I died," I finished for him.

"And you're... a god."

"Half."

"Half," he agreed.

"And your Uncle is also a..."

A nod.

"And what is his responsibility?"

Each God was endowed with a tremendous power that was entirely unique to them in exchange for the burden, and gift, of an equally great responsibility. As I had been endowed with the power to guide, and even control, souls. It also fell upon my shoulders to lead them into life beyond the known realms. It required a constant flow of my magic as my energy extended itself autonomously to them. Much like breathing, it wasn't a conscious effort. But it was such a massive undertaking that what magic remained for my own use left me only considerably more powerful than the average magically inclined immortal.

"He's responsible for humans, the sky, justice, etc..."

I couldn't stifle the sneer that overcame me.

"Justice?! Is that a fucking joke?"

Kyril chuckled, subtle confusion furrowing his brow.

"That almost sounded personal..."

I nearly cackled in fury and my words turned borderline maniacal in their bitter enthusiasm.

"Actually... There's something we need to discuss."

Kyril's eyes narrowed before flitting briefly to the gaudy monstrosity I assumed his Uncle called home before returning to mine.

My voice became a growl. "Rather urgently."

Kyril's brows drew down ominously, no doubt feeling through our tether the trepidation knotting my stomach.

"Your Uncle... That night in the tent... During the war..."

Kyril's gaze ignited, burning with increasing fury as realisation slowly creeped in... the puzzle pieces of our shared histories suddenly coming together. Everything that had led up to this moment. Namely, Kyril's uncle murdering me so that Kyril would help him collect the seals and open the doorway between realms. The reason as to why Caelus would want to do such a thing still evaded me.

But the words *burned* as they spilled forward.

"It was him."

Kyril held my gaze for a few moments.

The rage I felt swelling within him rose like a tsunami as he silently turned towards his Uncles's mansion that laid only a hundred yards or so in the distance.

Nuala and I exchanged worried glances in the stillness and silence.

Quetz, as usual, seemed entirely at ease, though his eyes were glowing again- the giveaway that he was travelling somewhere, or rather some time, outside of *here*.

The smell of burning wood drifted to me.

A loud groan sounded from within Caelus' manor and ended in a loud crack, splitting the exterior of the structure down the middle. Flames erupted at the first gust of wind.

Nuala and I stood, lips parting in shock.

Kyril's body trembled with rage and sweat beaded down the side of his face as his power unfurled around him and his prey- Caelus' massive home.

Quetz watched the house burn with an expression that could have led one to believe he were watching children play a game of chess and one of them had just made a mildly intriguing move.

. . .

As the fire grew and the structure of the house began to collapse, the tensing of Kyril's muscles began to relax.

"I'll be right back," he clipped. Kyril folded out of sight and after only a few brief moment's he returned with what remained of a silk bedsheet wrapped up and slung over his shoulder like a sack.

My stomach churned at the sight, intuitively knowing what it already held. The sigillums.

His eyes flicked to Quetz. "Do you know where he is?"

Quetz's eyes were still glowing brilliantly, like twin turquoise seas radiating beneath the sun before his brows drew together, a small frown tilting his lips.

"... No. He prevents anyone from seeing. His magic is... quite strong..."

Their words drifted into the ether as what felt like my chest was cracking open and my heart had been flayed and incinerated much like Caelus' home. The only solution there was, one that I'd been desperately pushing away from my reeling mind, reared forward as a knowingness settled into me.

He had all of the sigillums.

And while he hadn't enlightened me with how exactly he'd planned to conduct the ritual required to piece them together and open the doorway between dimensions...

Chaos and death were bound to descend. Just as Quetz had fore-warned. And I knew precisely the price of war. And maybe Quetz wasn't worried about the sigillums, for some bizarre reason, perhaps because he knew that I would never allow it. And that even though it would destroy me to stop Kyril...

To remove his soul from his body and kill *him. Sending him to the next dimension...* Quetz also knew that I wouldn't risk trillions of others to save myself from the agony.

I wanted to scream and cry and pound my fists into his chest. *How could he do this?* I turned to Kyril his lips pressing together in a grim line as though he already knew and had predicted this very outcome. He knew me better than that. To think that I'd ever allow him to do such a thing.

My voice cracked with the words. "Give me the sigillums, Kyril."

He closed the small distance between us and stared down into my eyes. I could feel the magic of the sigillums pouring over us in burning waves. "Don't do this. My Uncle will hunt you down. Let me protect you."

"This isn't about me. This is about the countless lives that would end because of you. You already know it would take no more than a thought for me to end his life..."

"And if he catches you off guard? Like he did 200 years ago. And like Lussathir did only hours ago."

Tears swelled. "Don't make me do this, Kyril. *Please.*"

Kyril's expression was filled with sad, grim resolve, softening as I reached up and took his face in my hands. I pressed my body against his and willed all my love for him through our tether.

His hands closed around my waist as he lowered his face to mine, hovering only a few inches away.

I stood on the tips of my toes, grazing the tip of my nose gently against his cheek as I spoke softly against him.

"Please... Don't do this. I love you. I love our friends... And I know you do too. I can't let you do this to them. Or to *us.* If you stop now, we can move passed this... But if you... continue on this path... things will never be the same. And I will not stand by your side while you destroy our world and everything in it."

Kyril's fingers pressed into my flesh in desperation as he brought his forehead to mine and closed his eyes, wincing as though he were in physical pain.

"I have faith that one day you will forgive me and come to appreciate all I've done."

Kyril drew his hand to my cheek, caressing it with his thumb, wiping away a rogue droplet of my emotion. I couldn't help but lean into it. And as I closed my eyes, relishing the feel of his warmth, his being, his *everything* one last time...

Something cold and metallic slid against my throat and clicked. Cutting me off from my magic instantly. *A palladium collar.*

THREE

AURELIA

My eyes burst open, mind blanking with shock. Quickly to be replaced with *rage*. Rage, horror, and betrayal like I had never known roared within me.

Before I could react, searing pain wracked my body, back arching. A blinding white light filled my vision as a cry tore from my lips. Soaring through the air above us, I caught sight of Caelus just before he slammed, feet first, onto the ground a few yards away from us.

"No!" Kyril roared as he folded away from me, presumably to murder Caelus. Amidst the pain, I could feel my consciousness slipping through my fingers as I tried desperately to maintain my grasp.

The sound of cracking bones followed by an inhuman roar sounded beside me...

I knew that sound... That voice.

Nuala's Chimera form.

I managed to hold a single thought. Caelus. Despite however futile, I had to try. My spirit's will took form and reached out like a fist- however faint- to grasp onto him. As it found him, I yanked on his soul- like ripping a piece of cloth free from it's bolt. But it only slipped through my fingers. A distant, deep laugh filled my ears beneath the roaring and clashing renting the air. I yanked again. Nothing. Caelus' voice filled my mind. *"Such beautiful jewellery your nexus gives you."*

Even if I'd had any words to give him, I knew they'd never reach him with this collar around my neck. His lightning left me, having realized I was no longer a threat.

Gentle hands followed by strong arms curled around me. I willed my eyelids to open.

Quetz.

His features were contorted with a fury and disgust like I'd never seen. Whorls of his magic, his essence, twisted and lashed out around him as if begging to be released- his corporal form warring with his incorporeal form for dominance- even seeping out of his eyes like churning mist and waves. If I hadn't been absolutely certain his fury wasn't directed at me, I'd have been utterly terrified.

His words came out an ominous inhuman growl. A voice I barely recognized. Power oozing forth.

"What would you have me do?"

My heart pounded heavily- partially at his fearsome image- the other from dread. But my voice was steady with grim resolve. "Take the sigillums." Still clutching me tightly against his chest, he extended a forearm and the sack of sigillums flew into his outstretched hand.

My gaze shifted to find Nuala leaping back up from the rubble. Her massive, razor sharp maw open wide and ready to devour Caelus just as his and Kyril's focus slammed onto us. Kyril and Caelus roared as the heaven's opened and lightning spilled from above, and Kyril's fire erupted from below ready to consume Quetz and I.

· · ·

Before either could touch me, a great, winged-serpentine beast appeared before me absorbing the blows. Having shifted, Quetz's tail coiled around my body and the world tilted on its axis before folding in on itself.

CHAPTER

FOUR

AURELIA

A plume of turquoise, blue, gold, and red overtook my vision. Quetz's tail coiled and tightened around me protectively as we crashed into a body of water. Holding me and the sack of seals aloft, the water surrounding us splashed like a tidal wave as something velvety brushed against my skin.

Quetz's tail loosened and released me as I looked down to find my body cradled in turquoise and gold wings.

My lips parted in awe.

I had never seen his winged-serpent form.

My gaze wandered up to find his snake's head- the size of a small house- staring down at me with glowing turquoise eyes. Smoke rising from its nostrils.

And a large, jagged scar- a wound of newly charred flesh- marred the right side of his scaled face. Even with the scar, he was breathtakingly beautiful.

My voice came out breathy with awe.

"*Quetz....*"

A slender forked-tongue loosed from it's mouth and licked up the side of my body and my face as it leaned in and gently nuzzled me, in response. With his eyes this large, I could make out the beautiful flecks of gold, white, purple, and blue that whispered through the turquoise.

But the charred skin of his wounds were hissing with smoke.

"You're hurt..."

Quetz gave another gentle flick of his tongue in response as my gaze worked over the rest of him. He was covered in burns. And it further fueled my rage. Muddled by an odd mixture of guilt and relief.

Guilt for having left Nuala but relief that at least, despite how furious I was with him, that Kyril wasn't alone to fight Caelus.

It reassured me that they at least had each other to protect themselves against Caelus whilst Quetz and I hid the sigillums.

Outside of me, Kyril was her closest friend for over 300 years. She'd known him even longer than I had. He'd even given her a home in exile after she'd slaughtered Emperor Orova and gathered her forces to form the resistance.

I pressed my hands against the smooth flesh of his scales and sent out a powerful current of my energy to heal his wounds.

The pupils of his eyes flared as he nuzzled his head against my hand and my energy that coursed through him. I scanned what I could see of his body amidst the sea waves, watching the wounds close and disappear. The only one that lingered was the one on his face. Perhaps that was where he had received the brunt of Caelus' lightning and had been aiming to kill to prevent us from fleeing with the sigillums. He had already killed me once, after all.

"Caelus won't defeat them, right?"

Quetz hissed his displeasure, jaws opening to reveal pointed fangs like ten foot tusks. Taking that as a 'no', the anxiety in me eased slightly. I looked around at our surroundings.

A thatched roof home laid in the distance. The sea we floated in, about half a mile away from the shore. I sat up further in the bed of feathers Quetz cradled me in.

"Quetz. Can you switch forms for me, please?"

He only stared a blank response, unmoving.

I tried to pull on his spirit. To give it a tiny tug. But the collar. My fingers wrapped around the front of it, tugging uselessly at it. Only magic could remove it. Which I currently had no access to. I tried for The Creators' Promise between us, the tether of it that connected us.

The next thing I knew, the icy water of the sea was enveloping me.

I saw the bedsheet sack of sigillums crash into the water beside me. I tried reaching out to grab it but it only yanked me deeper into the water's depth. Much too heavy to tow to the surface, I let it slip from my grasp and kicked towards the surface. The water felt like ice on what was left of my raw wounds that Caelus' bolts of lightning had gifted me with but... I looked at my hands, my arms.

They were mostly healed. Though a little... crispy. I turned to find Quetz, returned to his god form, treading water a few feet away. Calm as ever, if not a bit confused. A jagged scar running down the right side of his face- forehead to mid-cheek- and another, smaller one that cut into his top lip, made my worry and my rage blossom anew.

"Are you alright?"

Quetz nodded, sweeping his dark, unruly, wet waves out of his face.

"... It's hard for me to leave that form. To even think properly when I'm in it... Are you ok?"

"Yes, but the sigillums are currently sitting on the sea floor. We need to mask them so Caelus and Kyril, or anyone else for that matter, can't track them."

Quetz's eyes flashed for a moment before disappearing beneath the surface.

A radiant, turquoise glow swam drifting further and further away until it blinked out of sight. I looked around, swimming in place in the quite calm of the gentle sea waves. After several too long moments, I flicked a glance towards the bottom again. The water much too deep for the light of day to penetrate its depths.

Gradually, unease slid along my skin. Just as I was about to try and swim to shore to wait for him, having grown entirely too petrified of the sharp-toothed creatures my imagination told me were surely only moments away from devouring me, Quetz reappeared in front of me.

"Boo!"

"You asshole," I gasped, splashing him with water even as my tension dissipated a little more. He tossed his head back with laughter looking far too handsome and joyous considering the circumstances. Still chuckling, he pulled me into his arms. The feeling of his rumbling laughter against my back warmed my entire being and for a moment I couldn't help but chuckle either.

Cool grass replaced the water beneath my bare feet and the silk robe that Lussathir had given me when he'd kidnapped me was gaping open, plastering itself to my naked body. Its tie lost forever to the tide. Thankfully, it was a relatively hot summer's day on this side of the realm. Despite the frigid waters.

I pulled my robe closed and wrung the sea water from my hair as Quetz stepped away. Who I now noticed was completely naked. I yanked my gaze up to his face, and away from the long, thick, and not entirely flaccid length of him.

"Sorry," he said, sounding as though he were apologizing for something as banal as a lost spoon, "Another side effect of shifting forms."

I cleared my throat, shoving away any natural, *physical reactions* to the undeniably inspiring sight of him.

In a blink, he was dressed in that magnificent uniform of his- an enormous feathered headdress, loin cloth, ornate large golden jewellery, and the feathered-cuffs decorating his calves and biceps.

All of that in addition to the extraordinary chest-to-ankle tattoos depicting his feathered serpent form along with all the whorls and geometric adornments.

Dejavu and sadness hit me at once as a very similar memory rose to my mind. The last and only time I'd seen him naked, and boasting his 'god uniform', had been when I'd first freed him from the mirror he'd willingly allowed Kyril to trap him in.

For thirty-three years.

So he could be there for me in my darkest our. Bring me to my brother who had just died at my side, and plant the seed that would lead to us being bound by The Creators' Promise after I escaped Pauperes Domos.

Why he would ever do such a thing was beyond me. Especially considering I had a nexus mate. But, as time had revealed, there were far greater things at play than what I could fully grasp at the moment.

My brows leapt to my forehead as I took him in, looking like some Emperor of the Wild Gods.

"That outfit really never gets any less impressive," I chuckled. He hummed appreciatively.

"Why thank you," he said holding my gaze, eyes twinkling.

"So what'd you do with the sigillums?"

"Hid them in what the humans call 'The Mariana Trench'. Sealed it inside one of the mountains down there. And even if they did manage to find it, miraculously, they'd definitely get eaten and shat out, more than once, before getting past its inhabitants."

My brows leapt with intrigue. "The kraken or something?"

He chuckled. "No, no. These creatures make the kraken look positively docile by comparison. Would you like me to introduce you? They can be quite lovely once you get to know them. As long as you don't try to steal anything..."

I huffed a laugh. "Perhaps another time. I've also shielded our energies from being traced or scried. Just let me know when you'd like them to find us and I can remove it but... for now..."

I nodded, unable to find any words to describe the betrayal and anger I was trying to pretend *wasn't* currently searing my veins, or the tether of mine and Kyril's nexus bond.

And the guilt at abandoning Nuala to deal with him alone. They'd probably argue like siblings, as per usual, despite being the best of friends and saving each other's lives numerous times in various battles, and the war centuries ago. But them being together did ease the worry that Caelus would overpower them.

Quetz's gaze sank, lingering on the heinous piece of metal currently latched around my neck, his features flickering with the fury I'd witnessed back at Caelus'. His hand reached out and gently pulled it from my neck. I nearly wept as I felt the connection to my magic return, pouring through me like a waterfall of tingling energy.

Quetz's words were apologetic. "I'd recommend we hold onto it..." *Just in case we need it.* I nodded in agreement, swallowing the desire to burn it to ashes.

The collar vanished from his hand, his gaze shifting to the thatched roof house in the distance. A familiar encouraging grin returned to his face. My heart clenched painfully at the scar now pulling at his handsome features, from forehead to jaw.

"Shall we visit 'The Long Lost King of Caligo"?

I was so focused trying to quell my rage that I almost missed his words.

My jaw dropped.

"King Darcos?"

Quetz's crooked grin widened.

"The one and only."

Before I could react, he stepped in close and laid his palm flat in the centre of my chest.

I gasped sharply at the sensation of tendrils of blue-green and gold light licking up my entire body.

The remaining cuts and burns on my skin all but evaporated. The colorful light receding.

"Thank you...," I murmured a little breathlessly.

A gentle smile was his response before turning towards King Darcos's adorable thatched-roof home.

I reached out and grabbed his arm. "Wait... What about your face? I tried my best to heal it but..."

Quetz lowered his brows, tracing his fingertips along the scars, tendrils of light whorling in their wake.

Thanks to my magic, the scars had already sealed and healed. But his magic only managed to shift the hue from pink to pale beige. They still stood out several shades paler against his bronze skin.

"Hmmm... Strange..."

His look of concern shifted to a flash of excitement.

"Does it make me look cool?"

I gave a surprised laugh, patting his feathered-cuff bicep.

"Not only do you look cool, you look *dangerous.*"

I waggled my eyebrows for emphasis.

Quetz tossed his head back with another soul-warming laugh as we trudged through the sand together towards Darcos' home. The action alone made a little more of my tension ease.

Though it didn't take long for my anxiety to return.

"You're sure Kyril and Nuala are ok?"

'Yep. I can't peer in on Kyril or Caeulus but I can on Nuala. She's already bound Caulus. I'm waiting to see what unfolds next."

I halted in my steps. "Which could be...?"

Quetz's steps slowed as he took a deep breath trying to find the words.

"There are so many tiny variables that influence things. It's incredibly difficult to verbalise... But, as a highly reductive example, Caelus' closest neighbour is currently hunting pheasants as we speak. Phaesants that often wander near the border of Caelus' property. If his neighbour's wife calls him back inside, a gunshot won't go off and distract Kyril and Nuala for the moment Caelus needs to break his magical binding before Kyril can sever his head from his body so that he can carve out and burn his heart. However, if when his neighbour's wife pours the olive oil in the pan she's about to cook grilled cheese sandwiches in, and sneezes as she does so because a mote of dost that floats too closely, and she inhales it, causing a bit of oil to splash on the floor... then she'll slip and bruise her tail bone. She forsakes making the grilled cheese sandwiches to ice her tailbone. So she won't call her husband. And Caelus won't have the fleeting moment of distraction he needs to survive."

I gape at him, brows furrowing.

He huffs a gratified laugh. "Welcome to the chaos of the universe."

I quirk an eyebrow. "And what about this mote of dust? What makes it float over to her?"

Quetz sighed heavily, eyes flashing briefly. "She has a golden retriever whose tail wags excitedly nearby if the squirrel inhabiting the tree in their front yard scurries by... Which is then determined by-."

I palmed my face, shaking my head. "Ok, ok, ok. I get it... Good Gods. That's what you have to sift through every time we ask you about potentialities?"

He gave a short, slightly maniacal and exasperated laugh.

"It's not *always* so arbitrarily convoluted but... That, my darling Aurelia, is just the *tip* of the universe's chaos' dick. Although you can rest assured, as I mentioned earlier... there are some things that are inevitable. It's just a matter of how we get there. The chaos, as unfathomably chaotic as it is, does seem to be divinely orchestrated, because from what I've witnessed... Even the most tragic of events *ultimately* leads to something profoundly beautiful that benefits the whole... Even if it takes a while. But it's far beyond anything I'll ever be able to comprehend."

My lips parted as his words settled deep within me. Like a seed, planted. And something like hope began to blossom.

The look on my face must have said as much and it made him chuckle. I exhaled a heavy sigh still reeling from his shared knowledge.

"And I'm guessing you still can't illuminate any of these 'inevitables'?"

The smile that blossomed on Quetz's face held so much promise it made my heart skip a beat.

"Now where would be the fun in that?"

FIVE

AURELIA

By the time we approached the thatched-roof house, we'd already been sun-dried and thoroughly windblown. Between my long, tangled tresses and Quetz's unruly waves- the two of us probably looked like we'd traveled through a tidal wave to get here. And being dressed in nothing more than a sandy, salt-crusted robe, I felt a little self-conscious.

Quetz side-eyed me as I tried to finger comb my hair, lips tilting as he stilled my hands by gently grabbing one of my wrists. His voice filled with a tenderness that made my heart swell a little in gratitude.

"It would take a lot more than some sea water to mask your beauty, Aurelia."

I grumbled my displeasure, still fiddling.

"Easy for you to say. You look like you just stepped off your gilded throne."

Quetz hefted another laugh. Abs flexing with every joyous spasm. He threw an arm around me and kissed the top of my head as he pulled me into his side.

I looked up to find King Darcos was already standing on his

porch watching us, squinting in what appeared to be a melange of disbelief and confusion. Though I hadn't seen him in a couple hundred years. And it had been when I was in another body. Though there was a striking resemblance and I knew more than anything that he would recognize the feel of my magic.

Each immortal had an energetic signature, and you didn't have to even see them to recognize it.

Darcos looked much the same as when I'd last seen him in the Caligoan realm. Though perhaps a little older. Wearier.

Despite the coolness of his pale skin, slender features, and the sharpness of his Elven ears, he exuded a softness and a warmth that had always endeared me to him. A certain gentleness that was rare amongst immortals.

Caligo, where we had met, was not an Elven realm. In fact, as far as I knew, he'd been one of the only ones to have lived there. When he'd ruled over it, it had become a realm of exiles inhabited by immortals and other creatures that had either been cast out or forced to run away from their home realms.

I'd always wondered what had lead him to flee Lux Dyradalis and seek exile in Caligo but I knew all too well that the often painful memories behind such stories were better left in the past.

King Darcos' lips parted to reveal his still radiant smile as he rose to greet us despite my new, though strikingly familiar, form.

"You have no idea the joy it brings me to see you reincarnated."

He bowed at the waist before I quickly closed the last several feet between us and threw my arms around him.

"You have no idea the joy it brings me to see *you*."

He chuckled warmly, wrapping his long arms around me and stood fully, making my feet dangle off the floor.

A handsome middle-aged male stepped out of the front door. A soft smile tilting his lips. He gave me a courteous nod, eyes darting and widening at the sight of Quetz.

And his breathtaking costume.

After a few long moments of a good squeeze, Darcos set me back on my feet.I reached up to cradle his face between my hands. Chest swelling with gratitude that he was ok. Tears swelled in my eyes.

"I'm so glad you're ok... This is Quetzacoatl. One of my dearest friends."

Quetz beamed at Darcos and his friend, shaking their hands.

I had to bite my cheek to stifle the laughter rising at the way Darcos and Graham were staring, wide-eyed at Quetz. He appeared to be both astonishingly godly and otherworldly in his breathtaking beauty, but also astonishingly... Bizarre. Enough to questions one's sanity unless he'd just stepped out of a portal to the wild Feroxian Islands on Aeternia.

And their eyes said as much as they seemed to dart and roam over him and his ensemble.

Finally, Darcos managed to actually speak.

"I'm so happy to meet you. This is my husband, Graham."

After shaking Quetz's hand, Graham gave me a warm grin and opened his arms towards me, and I happily welcomed his embrace.

The four of us stood in Darcos' kitchen, each of us tasked with various dinner preparations as per Graham's instructions as we drank red wine. Darcos had given Quetz and me both the gift of our own guest bedrooms with ensuite bathrooms, along with some clothing that he'd been able to magically tailor for both of us.

I couldn't help but study Graham without feeling a pang of sadness.

He was remarkably handsome, and could be described as a well groomed and muscled silver fox. Who at the moment was dressed in a rather flattering pair of jeans and a plaid flannel button down shirt. But he was very clearly human. My heart cracked a little at their impending heartache...

Darcos, save for lethal violence, would outlive Graham by many centuries, if not millennia.

Darcos caught my gaze, as I felt my own thoughtful stare lingering a little too long on him, and I knew he didn't need to be a telepath to read my thoughts.

I swallowed a little guiltily.

"Will he consider drinking ambrosia?" I asked Darcos mind-to-mind. I could hear his sigh in my head.

"He's refused me so far."

"And how long have you been married?"

"Only 15 years."

"... Perhaps I could help guide you two back together if and when he reincarnates... If that's something you'd both want."

Darcos' head lifted to meet my gaze from across the kitchen's island, smiling softly with gratitude, as he chopped garlic with a deftness and skill that revealed he probably hadn't had any servants to cook for him in quite sometime. Perhaps even since he'd fled Caligo.

"Thank you, Aurelia. I'll bring it up with him... Where's Kyril? If you don't mind me asking."

My throat worked on a hard swallow, emotion welling up in my chest. I'd managed, so far, to silence the tether between Kyril and me. Though it did burn like all the fiery hells of the many underworlds. But at least I didn't have to bear witness to all of his tumultuous emotions, nor he mine.

And it had significantly improved my ability to desperately ignore all the pain I was experiencing on my own in regards to his betrayal and complete and utter descent into madness...

That he had hidden so fucking well.

For the most part... The more I thought about things... The more certain comments and behaviours seemed to add up.

What in the gods' names were we going to do?

Even if I were some kind of sociopath who didn't bat an eye at potentially getting all of our friends and trillions of innocents slaughtered...

The betrayal alone at him slapping that collar on me again... After I'd spent my entire reincarnation- with exception of these past few months since I'd escaped Pauperes Domos- forced to wear a magic-suppressing palladium collar as I slaved away in the crystal quarry and mines...

It was... nigh-unforgivable. I would never have fathomed that he would put his needs so far above mine that he would do such a thing to me. And had known that when the day came that I found out, that I would be so upset and recognize how inarguably *wrong* everything he was doing was... That I would be willing to save our friends, and the inhabitants of the nine realms, by pulling his soul from his body. He had actually anticipated it. There's no other reason he would have a palladium collar nearby enough that he could spirit it into his hands.

That was also in addition to the fact that he had tried to *burn* Quetz and me. I was his nexus mate. I couldn't fathom intentionally causing him pain.

And Quetz...

Even after everything Quetz had done for us, he'd still intentionally tried to hurt him. And succeeded. He'd been covered in burns just as I would have been had Quetz not absorbed the blows.

The same *God* that had willingly allowed Kyril to trap him in a mirror for 33 years so that he could one day swear to protect *his* nexus mate.

And while I imagine he only intended on stopping us from folding away and stealing the sigillums, and had known that we would fairly rapidly heal... There were some wounds that left scars even if you couldn't see them. And while I could safely assume the scars now marring Quetz's face were from Caelus' lightning... Kyril's actions had caused irreparable damage nonetheless.

I couldn't even bring myself to imagine what else he was capable of doing to prevent me from stopping him from opening the doorway between dimensions- short of killing me- because he seemed to be absolutely fine with everything else. The thought caused me to bite my cheek so hard it bled as my tears swelled.

And not only had he betrayed me and Quetz, he'd betrayed all of his closest friends and allies. We'd fought a war together. Countless battles. Had spent centuries at each other's sides. My mind reeled at this.

Truly, seeing my decapitated body having had its heart torn out and burned to then mourn my death for two hundred years had driven him to madness. Just as Caelus had planned.

Caelus, his own uncle had murdered me in my sleep, all so that Kyril will would be driven to help him collect the seven sigillums to open the doorway to the dimensions beyond, though I had no recollection of it, or where my spirit resided for two hundred years after my first physical death.

Well, the first as far as I knew. It was probable that I'd had other reincarnations I simply couldn't remember. The only question left was...

What was Caelus' justification?

What had driven him to this madness. Was there something missing?

Some other reason, outside of *me* that had driven Kyril to do this?

'This' obviously being in addition to Kyril also being so willing to potentially sacrifice countless lives throughout the nine realms once that doorway was opened.

Some exasperated noise, meant to disguise the sob trying to work its way up my throat, left me as I tried to muster a response for Darcos. He would know just as well I did, having been good friend's with Kyril before Darcos had left for Terrenea, that Kyril wouldn't change his mind.

The gravity of Quetz's gaze snapped me out of the downward spiral of my thoughts and emotions. He'd been speaking animatedly with Graham as he discreetly gave a tug on the tether of our Creator's Promise, prompting a burst of warmth to fill my chest. Of strength and solidarity. Reassurance. Love and care. It made the emotion within in me swell higher and I had to bite the inside of my cheek again to quell it. I quickly reached for my wine and took a large gulp.

"He's made some rather... unfortunate decisions as of late."

I was deeply grateful to speak mind-to-mind, knowing that otherwise the words would have been unintelligible and broken by my tears.

Darcos' brows knit together with concern.

I explained everything that had happened as succinctly as I could.

Darcos listened patiently, his expression growing more and more pained, until finally he came to my side and wrapped his arms around me. Tears spilled down my cheeks as I buried my face in Darcos' chest.

Quetz and Graham's conversation waned into silence.

"Why don't we go sit on the porch?" Quetz suggested to Graham. *Bless him.*

Despite my, thankfully brief, emotional breakdown, we managed to have perhaps the most joyous dinner I'd had in this reincarnation.

We spent hours eating some of the most delicious food and wine I'd ever had, and I'd laughed myself to tears. A much needed cathartic release.

As the group of us grew sleepy and our enthusiasm waned from exhaustion I found my heart swell to bursting with gratitude for the gift of their presence, their love, and our time together.

Darcos and Graham were speaking in hushed tones, giggling

between themselves like the lovebirds they were. My heart clenched in response, thinking of Kyril.

I turned to look at Quetz whose eyes were already settled on me. "They're still ok?"

I'd asked Quetz about a thousand times since we'd arrived.

His patience never diminishing.

Apparently, the neighbor's golden retriever *had* wagged its tail, causing a rogue dust mote to drift towards his neighbours wife's nose, who then didn't finish the grilled cheese because she needed to ice her tailbone, and was left with no reason to call her husband. Thusly, allowing Caelus's neighbor's pheasant hunting to be uninterrupted, causing a gunshot to go off, and Kyril and Nuala to be distracted for all of a millisecond, in turn giving Caelus his minuscule window of opportunity to break his binds and escape.

Quetz raised his hand to my shoulder, his thumb drawing soothing circles on my exposed shoulder.

"They're fine. They're staying at an Inn. No sign of Caelus. And they're both mildly reassured by the fact neither of them can trace us or our magic, assuming Caelus won't be able to find us either. Which he won't. I've checked. He won't find us unless we want him to find us. As long as we avoid Southern California."

I scrunched up my face in response. "Where?"

"Just some place in the southern part of the Northern Hemisphere of this realm. It's quite beautiful actually. But entirely too many... Metal horses."

I snorted, the tipsiness suddenly hitting me. "Metal horses?"

"They call them 'cars'."

I felt a remarkable combination of dubiousness and confusion.

"But... what do they eat?"

Quetzacoatl chuckled.

"Oil, technically."

I gave disgusted look.

"Ew. Just straight oil? As in olive oil? Or... ?"

That earned me a full-on giggle.

"No, actually. It's oil that comes from deep beneath the ground. Left behind by dead non-fire-breathing-dragons."

"What?!"

I cackled, drawing the attention of Dracos and Graham.

"Now I *know* you're fucking with me."

Quetz tossed his head back and laughed. We both began to laugh hysterically. He seemed nearly as tipsy as I did. Dracos and Graham chuckled at our contagious laughter, throwing us inquisitive looks.

"I'm trying to explain 'cars' to her. She asked what metal horses eat and I explained they eat oil from the ground... Ya know, the oil that the non-fire-breathing-dragons left behind."

Dracos and Graham erupted with laughter.

My laughter waned as more questions rose within my mind.

"But wait... What do you mean they left it behind? Where did it come from?"

"They're bodies, I guess."

My laughter dwindled as my confusion increased desperately trying to fathom such a creature.

"They're bodies???... But from which orifice?"

Quetz, Dracos, and Graham all began weeping with laughter and I couldn't help but join them despite my ignorance. I playfully slapped Quetz's arm.

"Tell me! I need to know! Did it come from their mouthes? Or their butts?"

The question only earned me more laughs, and *zero* answers.

To prove to me that these things were actually real, I found myself standing on a wide stone path staring at a shiny, white, box-like metal contraption with darkened windows. I frowned in disappointment.

"Is it dead?"

I certainly felt no life force coming from it.

Graham huffed. "I certainly hope not. It cost me £45,000."

I didn't bother asking what the equivalent would be in gold or aeternum crystals but it sounded like a hefty sum considering the chagrin in his tone.

For the first time in all the centuries I'd known Darcos, a mischievous grin split his innocent face.

"Wanna go for a ride?"

We climbed onto squishy leather seats. Quetz and I sat in the back while Graham and Darcos sat in front of us.

The car purred to life.

I let out a yelp as the top half of the contraption began to peel away, folding into some hidden space behind us. I watched, a little awed, as we rolled backward- like butter sliding off a baked potato before halting and turning to roll forward at an increasing speed.

Bright lights on the front of the car illuminated our tree-lined path. I watched Darcos and Graham exchange an excited look before Darcos pressed a button on some panel between them and music filled my ears. A haunting twinkling of piano keys sounded making a feeling of tremendous longing fill my veins. Longing for what, I wasn't quite sure but it was no less beautiful. I shifted my gaze, staring out in wonder, out at the lush, endless fields we flew by, illuminated solely by moonlight.

The wind whipped wildly at my long hair making me fist it in one hand.

Quetz's hand took mine in his and gave it a squeeze, palming me a tie for my hair. I drew his hand to my mouth and give it a chaste kiss in gratitude. I turned to find him watching me, ocean eyes twinkling.

"Is this magic?" I asked, words brimming with wonder.

A corner of his mouth tipped up.

"You could say that. A human type of magic, certainly."

Although I had no human blood in me, a feeling not too dissimilar to pride filled my chest at how far humans had truly come. The last time I'd been in Terrenea, they'd still been shitting in holes and chamber pots. Even in Aeternia we still rode horses. Although we did have the magic of folding.

I tied my hair back as we flew at increasing speeds. The wind too loud for us to speak over. Graham heightened the volume in the music just as the haunting music rose to its climax. I felt a pull to return my gaze to Quetz and a wave of profound gratitude for him filled me.

I was safe.

Palladium collar-free.

Sigillums safely hidden away.

I didn't have to murder my nexus mate in the process.

I was completely scar-free, all thanks to Quetz absorbing the near-lethal bolt that Caelus had struck.

I was here, reunited with Darcos for the first time in centuries, enjoying the newest luxuries of Terrenea.

He had tied his life to mine after waiting for me for 33 years being trapped in a mirror in a dungeon. The male had never even met me before. I had often wondered what it was he saw in all his visions and scrying that would lead him to do such a thing. If he'd been my nexus mate, it would have made sense. But he wasn't.

Whatever it was... He had shown me a selflessness and loyalty far beyond what I could ever possibly fathom from anyone.

I laid my open palm in the seat between us and Quetz wove his long, strong fingers with mine. My heart beat a little faster and swelled a little fuller. It had nothing to do with lust or romance, and everything to do with an unconditional, unwavering love and gratitude.

I woke to the feeling of strong arms slipping beneath my thighs and around my back. Quetz lifted me out of the car and pulled me against his chest. My eyes peaked open, still feeling a little tipsy, and now extremely sleepy.

He gave me that gentle, crooked grin of his. His voice sounding like the depth of the oceans, yet carrying the warmth of the sun.

"Sleep, Aurelia."

I felt compelled to resist but being tucked against the warmth of his chest, his heart drumming its soothing beat against me whilst being cradled in his strength... I drifted back under.

SIX

AURELIA

Sunlight peaked beneath the curtains of the cozy guest bedroom I awoke in. My eyes fell to the empty spot beside me on the bed making my heart sink at the sight of it, and Kyril's absence.

I had tried reaching out to Nuala with my mind on several occasions but found nothing, as I expected, knowing that we were on the other side of the world. All I could feel was her soul still safely tethered to her body. And I was much too furious to consider speaking with Kyril.

Anxiety sank its claws into me at the thought.

How would we ever get passed this?

I pulled myself out of bed, refusing to let anxiety maintain its grip, and made my way towards the shower. Some slow and steady breathing beneath the steady flow of its rain would help cleanse me of these agonizing emotions. Rejuvenate me.

I took my time, slowly scrubbing every inch of my skin with the heavenly scented cleansers in Darcos' guest shower until I felt like the horror of the past couple days- everything with KaLalaa, Aelia, and Lussathir... Or even the weeks prior with Madame Yiruxat and

Hotep. I hadn't had time to breathe and recover. It had been a journey of one atrocity and battle after another. As I finished, I eyed the large, clawfoot bathtub sitting outside the small glass room that made up the shower. The bathtub sat on a raised, mosaic tile platform that boasted a stunning view of the sea beyond Darcos and Graham's home. And it beckoned me.

A soft knock on the bathroom door pulled me from sleep. I sat up, surprised that I'd somehow fallen asleep in the bathtub. The water had even gone cold.

"Aurelia?" Quetz asked from the other side of the door.

"Hey- yes. Sorry, I fell asleep in here."

A brief pause.

"Good. I'm sure you needed the rest... I just came to check in on you. It's nearly two. Wanted to make sure you were feeling ok."

I rose from the water, sloshing it over the edge as I quickly grabbed a fluffy bathrobe and slipped it on before opening the door.

"Hey."

Quetz stared down at me, his mouth tilting upwards.

"Need anything?"

"No... Thank you though. For coming to check on me. And to wake me. Lest I drown."

"You know I'd never let that happen. Creator's promise or no."

My heart squeezed, throat working on a swallow.

"Same," I said in earnest.

Something drew tighter in the air between us. Whatever it was, I didn't want to acknowledge it.

As if reading my mind, Quetz stepped back and I felt my shameful heart dip in disappointment. "Perfect," he murmured before clearing his throat, speaking a little louder. "I'll... See you downstairs then. Unless you'd like to rest in your room. One of us can bring you what we set aside for you from breakfast and lunch."

"I'll be down in just a few."

I jogged down the stairs feeling relatively rejuvenated despite the gaping wound of Kyril's betrayal, and my anxiety and concern for Nuala. Graham, Darcos, and Quetz stood munching in the kitchen. All of them were dressed in, what I could only assume, was some kind of modernized human version of horseback riding attire.

Less than an hour later, Graham was handing me the reins to a beautiful, though apparently, geriatric gelding.

"I hear that it's been... a couple hundred years since you've ridden properly. Redmoon is about as docile and friendly as they come. Though he prefers to go at a... steady pace."

I chuckled appreciatively.

"Steady sounds ideal. It's been a stressful couple months... And I've only ridden once in this reincarnation."

Graham's eyebrows leapt towards his forehead, hesitating as I glided my hand over the muscled shoulder of the sorrel-colored horse, reaching out with my spirit to his in a soothing manner. He leaned into my touch in response, instantly making my heart warm even further toward him.

Graham's voice nearly became a whisper as he spoke.

"Do you think that... I'll reincarnate again?"

I lifted my eyes to his, a smile lifting my expression as I recalled my suggestion to Darcos the previous night.

"Probably. You most likely have already. Many times in fact."

Graham's eyes widened, lips parting and closing repeatedly as if he were struggling to find the words.

I reached out and gave his arm a reassuring squeeze.

"Should you choose to never take any ambrosia... I can try my best to reunite your soul with Darcos if you were to reincarnate."

Graham's eyes searched mine as he spoke. "And what if I were to reincarnate but he had already passed?"

I took a deep breath, unable to find words that were more reassuring.

"There's never any guarantee. So many things are beyond my knowledge. My power. I don't have any control of reincarnation but if I were to reincarnate, I could find you and help reconnect the two of you."

Graham's eyes seemed to dim.

"Is it possible for us to reunite when we are both passed?" I chewed my cheek... "If you're nexus mates... Then yes, certainly."

Graham nodded in understanding, a sadness settling over him. I could guess why but I dare not ask.

Quetz and Graham trotted over to us on their horses rescuing us both from the increasingly painful conversation. We spent the rest of the afternoon, and well into the evening riding along the coast, picnicking, and relaxing beneath the sun. It all seemed so dream-like and... surreal. Unlike anything I'd ever known. In this lifetime, I'd never known the freedom of... time and just existing. Enjoying something without some kind of potential doom rushing towards us.

Only a few months ago, I'd spent my days slaving away at the aeternam crystal quarry, living in a tiny slum with my brother.

Although, the lingering question of what would happen with Kyril, Caelus, and the sigillums that were now hidden in a trench deep beneath the sea still loomed....

And also the issue with the scheming rebel fae who *I'd freed* from Pauperes Domos were surely planning something...

But... at least it all wasn't *imminently* life-threatening.

Caelus and Kyril wouldn't be able to find us, and the rebel fae were on another planet in another realm far away from Nuala and me. I was surrounded by peace at *this* moment in some sort of peaceful stalemate.

It felt like we'd discovered a pocket realm that we could escape from reality from... For however brief. And outside of resolving the situation peacefully, which seemed an impossibility... I wanted nothing more than to stay here for as long as absolutely possible, existing in this haven of friendship, fun, and *rest*.

The four of us were laid out on large picnic blankets in the sand. Our horses, happily eating the nearby grasses beyond the sandy shore. Thoroughly fed and stuffed, Darcos laid back on the blanket and reached out for Graham, pulling him down into his arms.

Watching them was bittersweet.

I was happy for them. Especially for Darcos who deserved this *so* much after everything he'd been through, and it was beautiful to witness but...

It was also an excruciating reminder of what *wasn't* happening between me and Kyril.

Of everything he had done, and everything that we had lost because of it. How much he had hurt and betrayed me, and all of our closest friends.

It roused something bitter within me. Bitter and angry. I was furious Kyril had done this. And was *still* doing this. He had been utterly remorseless.

I felt as though my heart and soul had been put through a shredder not only from his actions but the fact that he was willing to hurt not only me, or even his closest friends, but bring so much suffering and doom to the realms, all so that he could protect himself from the potential suffering of losing me again if something were to happen. It made me feel like I didn't actually know him.

My *nexus mate*.

I couldn't even begin to fathom what he went through in those two hundred years after my death but... But it was clear that madness had descended him. His words returned to me.

"I would burn the world just to keep you with me."

"... Not even death *could keep me from you."*

My stomach suddenly roiled with nausea at the realization.

All this time... he had *told* me.

I had loved hearing it at the time. But I thought he'd meant it in a more *selfless* way that meant he would sacrifice himself to protect me. Just as I would him. But... I couldn't fathom sacrificing countless others to save only myself soul crushing grief by imposing it on others. As nexus mates, once we both passed, we would reunite in the dimensions beyond...

It made me feel like I'd rather be alone for the rest of eternity than be bound to someone who only knew how to love selfishly. Which... To me wasn't *really* love at all.

His actions and words had made me realize that everything he'd done throughout our entire relationship was to only protect and benefit him. Being a good lover and partner to me had benefited him because making me happy was fulfilling, sure, but only up until the point that it served his motivations.

He'd fucking kidnapped me, put a palladium collar on me, and even tried to cause me physical harm... Because I was no longer aligned with what he felt benefited himself. Throw in the fact he was actively *trying* to 'burn the world to keep me by his side'... *And* betray all of his closest friends and allies over the course of centuries...

Made me *murderous.*

And it also made me feel like everything we had was all a lie.

An illusion.

Warm fingertips grazed the back of my arm as I tried to stifle the emotion threatening to spill over again. I turned to look at Quetz whose expression was tightened with concern.

The look we shared said everything without having to verbalize anything, and communicated more than words could effectively express.

He was here.

He cared.

He had saved me and protected me so many times without ever asking anything in return despite having only met me mere months ago.

There was no sexual pressure or lust to cloud our heads, or the accompanying desperation.

Just clear, unwavering *loyal* love and support.

And that wasn't to say he wasn't insanely attractive... but...

I took a deep breath shoving the thought far away.

"Thank you, Quetz."

Quetz's expression, for once, remained serious. His eyes searching mine for another moment before he pulled me into his arms and laid back on the sand. I laid my head on his chest, curling my arm around his waist, draping a leg over one of his.

His arms pulled me tighter against him, and he kissed the top of my head in response.

CHAPTER
SEVEN
AURELIA

Quetz and I walked several feet behind Graham and Darcos carrying the picnic blankets after we left the horses in the fields to roam until the summer sun set.

They were so joyous and at ease with each other. I wanted to ask Darcos if they were nexus mates but I had a feeling I already knew the answer.

I turned my head to study Quetz... Wondering...

"Did you ever meet your nexus mate?"

Something seemed to dim within Quetz's luminous eyes before falling to the worn path in the grass we treaded. A sad, soft smile weighing down his expression.

"I did."

A knot of empathy, and something else that I felt too ashamed to name, twisted painfully in my stomach. I remained silent for a moment, not wanting to push the subject.

But I couldn't help myself.

"Where is she? He?"

Quetz sighed heavily as though recalling a particularly painful memory.

"*She* is no longer who she once was. *What* she once was."

My brows drew tightly together and something like dread wrung its fists around my guts.

"Do you mind me asking you what happened?"

Quetz flicked his eyes at me, flashing me an appreciative grin.

"Not at all... But we've had such a beautiful day. I wouldn't wanna ruin it with a depressing story."

I nodded my understanding guiltily even as I found myself asking one last question.

"When was the last time you saw her?"

"... Far too many years to count, and long ago enough that everything that happened then is nothing more than a greatly distant memory."

Ok, maybe *one* more question.

"Do you miss her?"

Quetz stopped in his tracks and returned the pale twin emeralds of his gaze to me, a mischievous grin finally returning to his face.

The look alone nearly made my knees buckle. Both at seeing his sadness evaporate, and simply at how breathtaking he truly was. Gods help *anyone* who stood on the other end of that gaze.

"Why do you ask, Aurelia?"

My cheeks practically burst into flames.

"Wha- I-... I-.... Obviously, I would just imagine that-"

Quetz stepped forward, directly *in* to my personal space, effectively making my breath catch and my heart to throw itself furiously against its cage. Whether to escape him or to throw itself at him, I was entirely unwilling to investigate.

Utterly at ease, he leaned in a little closer to me, searching my gaze as if for the truth that he knew my words wouldn't give. His deep voice, otherworldly in its power and perfection, had definitely lowered an octave.

"Would it bother you if I did?"

My mouth, that had been hanging slightly ajar, snapped shut at the realization it had gone completely dry. My tongue slipped between my pressed lips to wet them and I was suddenly *parched* in more ways than I dared to admit.

His eyes tracked the movement, pupils flaring wide, grin broadening.

Something coiled deep within me and began to seep a tingling heat through my body. And it made me *gulp.*

"So responsive."

I wasn't sure if he was speaking to my body betraying me, or was being facetious because of the words that failed me.

But much to my own surprise, my lady balls decided to make a rather bold appearance.

I found myself leaning toward him in a challenge, unable to suppress the feline grin twisting my lips.

"Would you like it if I was?"

My heart continued to pound in my chest but I found my magic rising in excitement.

Quetz's grinned mischievous grin softened to something sweeter as he brought his fingers to my cheek. His words disarming me entirely with their gentleness and sincerity.

"I wouldn't ever want you to experience something as painful as jealousy, especially not on my behalf. But it would bring me tremendous satisfaction to know that you cared."

Oh my.

Oh my, my, my…

The heat that had been coiling deep within me burst into flames and rose like a fan to a furnace.

We were still standing halfway between the stables and Darcos' house. The burgeoning emotion swelled with in me, threatening to swallow me whole. So I promptly shoved it away.

Unable to withstand the gravitas of his gaze, my eyes drifted to Darcos and Graham who were just walking in the backdoor of their house. Darcos glanced back at us, grinning a little sheepishly.

Knowingly.

As he shut the door.

The question left my mouth before I thought twice about it.

"Would you like to go back to the beach? ... I don't think I'm ready for this day to end yet."

Quetz answered with one of his lopsided grins as he offered me the crook of his elbow.

We laid on the blankets in the sand in companionable silence until the stars twinkled into existence above us. I was tucked tightly against Quetz's side as he held me to him. An involuntary shiver worked through me as the wind became a chill.

Quetz rolled onto his side tucking me against his chest before he pulled one of the blanks over me, cradling my head between his bicep and his other hand.

I felt my eyes close and as I did, the stars surrounded us as though we stood in the centre of the universe. Distant galaxies peppered an infinite horizon looking as though the hand of the creators had painted cotton candy and stars onto an endless blanket of darkest night and velvet.

I stood in awe, half tempted to try and reach out and touch it. It all seemed so close.

A warm, large hand slipped into mine and curled long fingers around it.

My gaze drifted to the male standing beside me. His eyes glowed and sparkled like sea green emeralds illuminated from within.

The tension in my chest further loosened and relaxed until it seemed to drift away entirely as my gaze returned to the stars and galaxies around us. My eyes wandered, like my mind, visiting each one briefly.

"How many realms outside of our own have you visited?"

Quetz paused for a moment taking a deep breath. His lips pressed together as if recalling something painful.

"More than I'd ever wanted."

He'd said it with such sadness, my brows drew together with concern and surprise. His only elaboration a sad smile. And although I wanted to ask what he meant, I wanted him to enjoy this time together more.

So I changed the subject.

"Which one's your favourite?"

And my heart nearly burst in relief because of it.

His full mouth split a feline grin. Looking like he knew some great secret I'd yet to discover as he pulled me into his side, craning his neck down to gently kiss the top of my head.

"That depends."

"On what?"

The next grin he gave me was nothing short of smug as he hummed with a certain satisfaction.

"I'll tell you one day. But that day is not today."

I furrowed my brows briefly wanting to push but... I could hardly muster the desire being surrounded by so much beauty. So much possibility.

"Have you seen what happens if he opens the doorway between dimensions?"

Quetz' eyes became distant. His grin fading.

"No."

I couldn't bite back my surprise.

"Why?"

Quetz's demeanour seemed to darken further.

"I don't have to. I was there the first time."

Shock filled me.

I'd known that he was from another dimension... I just... Didn't realize he'd arrived here so long ago. That he was one of *the originals.*

It had happened thousands of years ago. What little written history there was from back then was little more than conjecture outside of the few bits of literature that had survived. All we really knew was that they bore tremendous power and had come from... *elsewhere.*

And once they arrived, they'd enslaved the masses and wreaked destruction. The Seven Seals, or Sigillums, of The Nine Realms had been born in the dimension they'd come from. They'd been given as a gift to the first empress of the nine realms. A half-fae who was the daughter of one of the inter-dimensional entities that had first opened, and closed, that doorway.

But perhaps that's what gave Kyril his misguided confidence. We had fought in the war against the distant descendants of 'the originals' to have come here.

And won.

I had so many questions I barely knew where to begin.

"What made you want to come here in the first place?"

Quetz's gaze roamed the galaxies with the weight of an anvil and it made me regret even asking the question. But still he answered.

"I didn't."

He heaved a great sigh as though bracing himself for the memory.

"It was an accident... I'd been drifting aimlessly through the verses for eons in a form that could only be described as something between spirit and... a vague consciousness. A fragment of it. Just... existing. And as though pulled by some invisible hand through universe after universe for a period of time longer than the mind of man can conceive, my soul- if that's what it could have even been called- was drawn through that doorway. And I've been here ever since.

"So no, I haven't looked to see what happens if your nexus opens the doorway. I was here the first time it opened, and as I drifted through more universes than even I can count, I became witness to a great number of realms that thought it wise to open themselves to beings outside their realms, their dimensions. I've seen entire galaxies drained of the energy of all their suns and stars in an *instant*. And while I was also gifted to witness other benevolent beings create whole *new* universes... I know it's not worth the risk."

I'd craned my neck to look up at him wholly blown away by everything he'd said as my mind spun trying to fathom it... Beings that built whole *universes*...

And Kyril... how could I ever convince him that by opening that doorway we could meet the makers of our doom when we had won one war against them already... Against their descendants at least.

As insignificant it was in the grand scheme of things, the realization still made my heart sink even further... Because if he didn't change- which started with him not wanting to open that doorway... Then there truly was no hope for any future Kyril and I might have had together.

The stars around us faded and I found myself still curled up against Quetz's chest. A sense of hopelessness and despair settled on my chest.

I sat up, facing the sea, having to consciously force steady, slow breaths in and out of my lungs because I felt like screaming.

"I'm going for a swim," I heard myself say, dully.

Quetz remained silent as I stood and made my way towards the water, quickly peeling off my clothes, piece-by-piece, as I went. Liberating myself of the last shred of my clothing, relief filled me as I ran and dove into the sea waves that hungrily swallowed every inch of me that I was more than happy to give.

Despite the darkness, the further I swam out the more peace and relief I felt. Each stroke fuelling a cathartic purge until I was so far from the shore, I could barely make out Quetz's silhouette standing in the shallow water.

Watching.

Waiting.

Protecting.

Ever patient and unwavering.

I sent him a silent 'thank you' and allowed myself to float on the surface of the calm water, staring up at the blanket of stars above. Breathing through the last of the fiery anguish burning the tether of the nexus bond between Kyril and I that the cold kiss of the sea hadn't yet washed away.

And gradually the burning of our tether faded and my flesh grew numb, and my limbs too heavy to swim. I finally made my way back to shore, where Quetz was standing sentinel, ever patient, on the shore.

Slightly rejuvenated, I trudged my naked body back onto dry land.

Quetz folded out of sight to return a breath later holding a fluffy robe. As my body rose above the modesty the waves offered me, his gaze fell to the sand. I couldn't help the grin his bashfulness painted on my face. Especially considering he'd had *zero* qualms with prancing around naked, however accidental. Though no one could blame him.

I had to chew the inside of my cheek to stifle my smug grin.

"I didn't realize my nudity caused you so much discomfort."

Quetz's gaze flicked back up to mine. Not bothering at all to stifle the cat-like grin stretching across his own face. "*Discomfort* is hardly the word I would use to describe what your nudity does to me."

And with that he turned and walked away to gather the picnic blankets. I blinked, standing in the hazy stupor his words had left me in.

A gust of wind whipping against my cold, naked body snapped me out of my daze. I quickly bundled myself up in what I could now smell to be *his* bathrobe. I brought the lapel of it to my nose and inhaled deeply, feeling a *little* self-conscious, and a little more creepy.

But clearly not enough that it would prevent the butterfly in my stomach from giving a heavy flap of its wings. Although I immediately shooed it away. Obviously.

He smelled like warm summer rain, jasmine, and sandalwood.

EIGHT

AURELIA

"He looks like some tattooed, villain, mastermind from James Bond meets... some kind of Amazonian God," I heard Graham breathe as I closed the door to my bedroom.

I descended the stairs to see Darcos' eyes slowly sliding to his husband's, a knowing smirk painting his face. "Is that so?" Darcos questioned coolly. "What?" Graham shrugged, his handsome face now turning rosy as their gazes shifted to mine.

"Oh my...," Darcos awed as I came down the stairs.

I bit the inside of my cheek as I approached them. Both dressed in impeccably tailored suits. Darcos in dark blue, Graham in a kind of dark blue and grey plaid wool. Each with a splash of colour stuffed in their breast pocket. Darcos' pointed ears had been glamoured to look human for the evening, an inconvenience neither Quetz or I had to deal with.

"You are breathtaking in that dress, love," Graham added.

Darcos had let me procured a long, glossy silk gown of emerald green that had a deep cowl neckline, revealing the valley between the swell of my full breasts. The back of the dress had a matching cowl exposing the entirety of my back, and settled just above curve of my bum. The rest of the dress spilled to the floor.

When I'd looked in the mirror, my heart had clenched, thinking of Syan and how she'd made me a similar dress when I'd first arrived at Nuala's palace, for the Summer Solstice celebration, shortly after I'd escaped from Pauperes Domos.

I sent a silent prayer to The Creators that she was doing well.

"Thank you. You both look *wildly* dashing."

The two of them would surely be the envy of everyone at the restaurant we were going to tonight to celebrate Graham's birthday. I stepped up to him and stood on my tip-toes to lay a kiss on his cheek as I slid two silk-wrapped gifts into his hands. "Happy birthday, gorgeous one." I'd briefly folded back to the Aeternian Realm, to visit the Southern Guard's capital to procure a couple gifts for him.

Graham released a manly squeal of delight.

"Ooooh! Do you mind if I open them now?"

"Please, do."

He opened the first, and smallest one: a ring that would enable him to levitate things. He gushed over it, and then promptly shattered a vase. Before using it to quickly lifts its remnants into the garbage.

The second brought tears to his eyes.

A book entitled, 'Darcos Elian: The Benevolent King of the Exiles'. I knew that, as an exile, Darcos likely never risked leaving Terrenea lest he be found. Although now that KaLalaa had died at Eleni's hands perhaps he would one day return...

I'm sure that Darcos had told him loads about his history but it was a different thing entirely to hear, or read about it, from another perspective. From *history books*.

He swept me into his muscly arms, lifting me off my feet. I let out a squeal in surprise, wrapping my arms around his neck to return his embrace.

"Thank you, Aurelia."

. . .

I turned to find Quetz standing behind us. His short but unruly black waves tamed and combed back in a way I'd never seen him wear it. The darkest green suit he wore was perfectly tailored to fit his tall, muscled form, and was decorated with a golden snake brooch pinned to the lapel. He'd left the top two buttons of his shirt undone, gifting us all with a peek of the tattooed muscle beneath. Although I was unfamiliar with this style of fashion, he looked no less... breathtaking.

Quetz's lips parted as his gaze roamed over me. My throat worked on a swallow feeling a tension in the air that I had no business acknowledging.

I broke whatever trance had blossomed between us and stepped towards him, pressing a chaste kiss to his cheek.

My voice sounded far more nonchalant and steady than I felt.

"You look phenomenal."

His deep voice resonated through me even though he spoke softly.

"Thank you..."

I ignored the pang of disappointment I felt when he didn't return my compliment, suddenly feeling slightly self-conscious in this revealing dress. I tugged at the neckline trying to cover my cleavage a little more as I forced a smile.

Either he recognized the action for what it was, or he felt it through our tether, because he leaned into me and spoke in my hear so that only I could hear.

"You rendered me speechless, Aurelia. Words can't describe your beauty. Both the inner, and the outer, that you exude."

Now who was speechless. A moment passed where he lingered at my ear, my cheek. And as my heart sung a song that I'd learned only he could inspire, I lingered with my head tilted up into the crook of his neck.

I studied the smooth, bronze flesh there. Absently waiting for words to come that clearly wanted nothing to do with me. He had a small constellation of tiny freckles that seemed to form the shape of a comet. And hovering in this beautiful, peaceful corner of the worlds- of him- drew an almost painful longing for me to lean in and kiss that freckled comet.

But my conscience promptly swore at me. Rightly so.

I pulled back slightly, feeling a pang of remorse as I did. Our eyes met and all I could whisper was a barely audible 'thank you'.

A small, knowing smile perched itself on the corner of his full mouth but, mercifully, he didn't say anything more to stoke the flames of the tiny fire he'd started inside my chest. And on my cheeks.

Before he could think better of it, I quickly turned to face Graham and Darcos who were even quicker to look anywhere but at us and pretend they hadn't been thoroughly entertained.

My voice came out a little louder, and far shakier, than I'd intended.

"I take it we're riding in your metal horse?"

The drive to the restaurant was... interesting. The further we drove from Darcos' house, away from countryside/seaside, and into the town near where he lived, the more I realized just how startlingly different Terrenea was from the other realms.

Everything seemed to buzz with electricity. In the crowds and densely populated areas, the thicker the scent of burning oil filled the air. Metal replaced wood and stone. Electricity replaced aeternum crystals, fae lights, and fire. Humans had truly become something... other. It vaguely reminded me of what Caligo had become after Darcos fled and KaLalaa ruled.

I couldn't help but wonder if one got their inspiration from the other.

The most familiar thing I discovered, surprisingly, was the restaurant Graham explained the style of architecture and design was called 'Art Nouveau' but to me it nearly looked like something straight out of Lux Dryadalis- the realm of light elves.

Where Darcos had originally been born.

I couldn't help but grin, imagining how some of them *must* have had an influence here. Their designs and aesthetics were truly some of my favourite. A tall ceiling with sweeping arches embellished with crown molding and sculptures inspired by nature- twisting vines, blossoming flowers, flowing water.

Each column in the room was sculpted to depict nude towering goddesses baring lanterns that emitted a glowing amber light. Live music played, music that Darcos referred to as 'French Jazz'.

Whatever it was, it made me fall in love with this moment. A seed was planted in my mind as we sat in squishy velvet seats peppered around a round table that matched mine and Quetz's outfits.

Perhaps until Kyril and I sorted our madness out, I could stay in Terrenea for a while. Or even Lux Dryadalis. It had always been so beautiful there. And now that Eleni was Empress of the realm, I was certain life there would only improve.

But my hope was swiftly stabbed by heartbreak at the thought of Kyril. I missed him terribly... Or at least who I thought he had been. I felt truly hopeless when it came to him. And the burning, twisting sensation of our tether told me it felt it too.

Having felt my emotions through our tether, Quetz slid his hand into mine and gave it a squeeze, briefly turning away from his conversation with Graham and Darcos.

"You ok?"

I nodded, pushing away my twisted mess of emotion.

"Was just admiring everything here... Was thinking about maybe... Staying in Terrenea for a little while. Or even Lux Dryadalis. Until things blow over with Kyril... Hopefully, without killing him."

Graham stopped mid-sentence in his conversation with Darcos

as his gaze leapt to mine.

"Hey! No talk of anything depressing! I know it's not easy to ignore everything going on but you still have every reason to enjoy yourself. So at least while you're here with us, we're celebrating. And whether that's just for tonight or for eternity- I'm not giving you a choice in the matter. You're going to enjoy yourself whether you like it or not."

I couldn't help but chuckle appreciatively. Both at his warmth and his words that inspired me to let go of what was beyond my control, and enjoy these precious moments.

I reached for my paloma spritz: a delicious, sour, fizzy drink Quetz had recommended I try. For which I was eternally grateful.

"To enjoying ourselves. Whether we like it or not."

Quetz held up his glass, a darkest amber liquid swirling within as Graham and Darcos joined.

"To Graham and Darcos hosting us, and inspiring us *to* enjoy ourselves."

Quetz's eyes twinkled as they met mine. The scar on his face still hadn't disappeared on his face but...

I'd begun to grow attached to it. Not that I wished it wouldn't heal but it was a physical representation of everything he'd done for me... And it did add a certain edge to his stunningly beautiful features that suited him.

Another swell of emotion filled my chest and I had to force myself to break his gaze. Again, trying to push this *feeling* away.

Quetz pulled out a tiny bottle of glowing elixir from his breast pocket and passed it Graham. "Happy birthday, darling."

Both Graham and Darcos' eyes widened at the sight of it.

"It's a healing elixir, should you ever need it. It refills on its own as soon as you drink it. It also reverses ageing slightly. Nothing major. Five to ten years."

Graham's and Darcos' eyes glistened with gratitude. Quetz's lips tipped, appreciative of their reaction. Graham's watery eyes darted between the two of us, voice croaking.

"You guys are just the best."

I felt another swell of emotion rise within me and I nearly cursed in exasperation at myself. These mercurial tidal waves of ardour were genuinely becoming cumbersome. My eyes stung and as they shifted to Quetz who met mine in synchronicity... A tear slipped down my cheek. *Fuck.* Was it too early to blame it on the tequila in my paloma spritz?

Quetz simply smiled and slipped his hand into mine, giving it another squeeze in solidarity just as Graham and Darcos clucked their tongues in unison, both rising from their chairs so we could all embrace.

I'm sure we looked a bit over the top to everyone else in the restaurant but I was passed the point of caring. I gladly took them in my arms, pressing firm kisses to their cheeks.

As the evening progressed and the flowing alcohol dissolved the last of our fellow patrons inhibitions, the music transformed from pleasant dining background music to something that beckoned your soul, and your hips to sway. People began to dance, laughter became uproarious, and soon the four us found our way to the crowded dance floor.

I followed behind Graham and Darcos, Quetz tailing me. The four of us weaving through the crowd hand-in-hand.

When we reached the centre and carved a small area for ourselves, dancing as a group. My heartache lifted with each step, sway, and gyration.

A smile took root and stayed, blossoming wider and wider.

But when the music slowed, the lights dimmed, and Darcos and Graham naturally partnered for an intimate song... It left me with Quetz. And my smile faltered with slightly nervous energy.

I couldn't help but take notice of the surrounding women cutting glances, or even blatantly staring, at him. I couldn't blame them. To say he was, without a doubt, the most attractive male in the room was a gutting understatement. His beauty was... nothing short of breathtaking.

And on top of all that, he had a certain selfless and endearing lack of self-seriousness that only added to his beauty. There was a humility to it.

His smiles that were so easy, generous, and playful never failed to encourage you. The way his eyes glowed and glittered with the warmth of the sun. The silky waves and curls of his hair, rarely hindered by any efforts to tame them, were as buoyant and free as he was, and made him look slightly mad in the most charming of eccentric ways. His enthusiasm and sincerity infused every word he spoke, increased by his animated gestures and facial expressions.

Everything about him welcomed you, and beckoned you to unburden yourself of everything that weighed you down. To share in his lightheartedness and joy. And when something did need to be taken seriously, he approached it with such loving tenderness and unwavering devotion...

Music slowing, Quetz and I naturally turned to each other. My heart leapt, stomach fluttering. All in the anticipation of being so close to him. To experience the feel of his tender touch.

Despite everything Kyril had done, and was currently doing, a stab of guilt filled me as I thought of him. How insanely *wrong* it was for me to have these blossoming, and utterly uncontrollable reactions towards Quetz.

Time seemed to slow as he met my gaze, offering his hand, and in slid mine. He gently pulled me against him with a look and a smile that said, *'I know you're hurting and you're scared but it's ok. I'm here. Just for you.'*

A slow latin rhythm curled around us. Our chests, pressed against one another, as he folded an arm around my waist as his free hand held mine. Our hips came together, weaving their own synchronized harmony as my legs wove between his. We slid across the dance floor as though this was something we'd always done, as though our bodies remembered the words our minds couldn't to a song sung long ago.

Everyone around us faded out of existence, along with every other concern in the world. Our breaths came in synchrony, like everything between us. My breasts pressing against his firm chest and diaphragm with oscillating degrees of pressure that made something deep within me tingle. His lips feathered against my forehead, occasionally dipping to my ear in our varying movements. Each time it made the warmth already blossoming in my core, that I was desperately trying to ignore, progressively unfurl. My heart thumped heavily against my chest in a way that had nothing to do with the exertion of our dance and everything to do with the male holding me.

As the music approached its crescendo, one of Quetz's hands slid down my waist, beyond my hips, and over my thigh. My leg rose to curl around his waist and my breath caught before unfurling in an ecstasy that nearly caused my eyes to roll so far into the back of my head, I felt a spark of gratitude they didn't get lost. Every single hair on my body rose as if even they were desperate to to touch him.

Quetz's eyes returned to mine as the arm holding my hand, swept across my back to brace me. Effortlessly, he lowered me until I was parallel with the ground. Just as my dress slid up to reveal my thigh, and nearly entire bum, Quetz's free hand grasped the wanton fabric and anchored it to my thigh. The words thank you approached the tip of my tongue but I was so entranced they never reached him. Still, his lips quirked knowingly before he pulled me back upright against him as the climax of the song spilled forth before beginning its descent.

I laid my head against the hard, yet oh-so-welcoming, plain of his broad chest, our bodies swaying slowly to the drifting rhythm. My mind reeled at what had just transpired until the song reached its end. The both of us hesitated to separate and when we did, our eyes met again and we both knew something had changed between us.

Graham's warm, gravelly voice snapped us out of our stupor.

"Wow. Remind me later to beg you both to teach Darcos and I to dance like *that*. Fucking hell, that was intense."

Feeling a little sheepish, I glanced around at what had become something of an audience. Although most had returned to their meals or their dancing, their gazes still lingered.

Darcos was grinning but I could tell he had the same questions I did. Probably in regards to Kyril, who he knew and liked. Or well *had* liked. Before everything he'd done. Although I'm sure he felt some semblance of loyalty to him. Not to mention, Nuala, since they'd had a casual fling after I'd freed him from the dungeon and he'd sworn The Creator's Promise to me. Shame tinged my already flushed cheeks as I took a deep breath to steady myself.

Graham, bless him, seemed to sense this and was quick to shift our focus, quickly stepping towards Quetz.

"Why don't you show me some of those moves?"

Darcos took a deep breath and pulled me towards him as the music started up again, smiling softly. Knowingly.

The words poured out of my mind into his, hotly fuelled by my shame.

"How terrible am I on a scale of 'understandable' to 'kindly remove your person from my presence before your wickedness burns us to the ground'?

Darcos' chuckle rumbled against my chest unwound some of my tension.

"There was nothing terrible about it. Quite the opposite in fact. I'm just worried about you."

I loosed a breath I was pretty sure I'd been holding since Quetz's arms had left me and in its wake reality had come crashing back.

"What do I do, Darcos? I... I can't be with someone who's willing to start another war just meet his self-serving agenda while betraying his friends and me to the point of even physically harming us... and I swear to The Creators that another palladium collar is never touching my throat again..."

Darcos rubbed my back in soothing circles as we continued to dance, though my efforts were now half-hearted. I anchored my forehead to his chest feeling so helpless in the situation. Torn emotionally. And still furious with everything Kyril had done.

"So don't. There's actually nothing you can do in this moment. Relish the fact. If being married to a human has taught me anything... It's that life is fleeting. When gifts such as joy, peace... love... find you-you cherish the fuck out of them. No matter how long, or how little they last."

I felt a little more of my tension release as I absorbed his words.

"And what about Quetz? I don't know what's happening but... Whatever it is, I feel like it's wrong. Kyril... he's my nexus for the gods' sake... And he's been with Nuala... How is this even happening?"

Darcos hesitated for several moments to speak. *"Regardless of Quetz... I would go as far to say that I once loved Kyril as a friend long before any of this... And I can hardly fathom what he went through in losing you at the hands of his own uncle but... I think that Kyril, with all the deception that had to take place in order for him to get this far into his machinations, sealed his fate long before he put that palladium collar around your neck."*

The rage I'd been feeling since we'd arrived seemed to shrivel as it was replaced with the anguish at the truth of his words.

"As for Nuala," he continued gently, *"Would this be the first time you've shared a male?"*

"No... but I know that she likes him a lot."

"Likes him as in... Loves him?"

Her words from mere weeks ago echoed in my mind... *'... I don't think I've ever been fucked so well in all my 400 years... And while there's definitely more than that... I don't think he's my nexus or anything...'*

I couldn't help but give a chuckle recalling them, in spite of my sadness.

Darcos drew a hand up to caress my hair as he spoke.

"You and I both know Nuala, and like most immortals, she's incredibly liberal about these things unless it's regarding a nexus mate... As we all know, life gets messy. And that's ok as long as your honest about it... As for Quetz, I hardly know him well enough to make any sort veritable judgement but... if I were to base my judgement of him on his actions... On everything you've told me he's done for you... It would be an absolute sin if I told you to forsake the possibility..."

After the song ended, I excused myself to use the bathroom and by the time I returned, Quetz was sitting alone at our table. Darcos and Graham still dancing amongst the crowd.

Quetz caught sight of me and stood. His eyes seemed to rove over me with unmistakable concern as I approached, stopping just in front of him. He'd stuffed his hands in his pockets but took one out to tuck a rogue wave behind my ear as he leaned in so he didn't have to shout to be heard. He could have spoke mind-to-mind but I couldn't help but relish the soothing depths of his voice.

"You ok?"

I nodded against him, his hand lingering against my cheek.

"I told Graham and Darcos that we were both tired..."

I pulled back to meet his gaze, feeling no small amount of gratitude to him that I now no longer had to pretend to be in the mood to celebrate, and found myself wincing with relief.

"Oh, thank the gods."

He chuckled, drawing something from his pocket, before he dangled a set of odd looking keys in front of my face.

"Darcos gave me the keys to the car."

My heart gave a little leap at the mischievous smile that danced on his lips.

CHAPTER
NINE

AURELIA

Uncertainty, and admittedly a tiny bit of fear, had me hesitating as Quetz held the car door open for me. "You're sure you're capable of controlling this thing?"

Quetz hummed smugly as he raised an empty hand only for a small glossy card with a tiny picture of him on it to appear. I squinted my eyes at it trying to read the tiny letters in the dark.

"It's what humans call a 'license', and it proves exactly how capable I am of 'controlling this thing'."

I frowned dubiously. Even as I sat down in the car and he leaned over me to strap me into the squishy seat.

"How does that card prove anything?"

"Because it means I took a test," he retorted very matter of factly before shutting the car's door. His reassurance only inspiring more questions.

"You took a test?" I pressed as he climbed into the seat next to me.

"Of course not, why would I ever bother to do such a thing?"

I snorted my laughter, palming my face. "You are..."

The car purred to life as he chirped. "Wonderful?"

I rolled my eyes, giving him the fakest scoff I think I'd ever feigned, pretending he wasn't exactly that.

"More like *devious*."

His deep chuckle warmed my soul and soothed the ache in my chest. As it always had. *"Ooh,* that does sound terribly exciting. Shall I stop?"

A wry grin twisted my lips. *"Don't you dare."*

We both threw our heads back and cackled as he guided us backwards and drove off. My laughter quickly waning as the speed he chose proved to be far less exciting than I'd anticipated.

"Doesn't it go a little faster? We were flying just the other night."

He slipped a hand over my knee and gave it a squeeze.

"Yes, but these creatures are dangerous if you give them too much encouragement. I wouldn't want to risk you getting hurt just for a bit of fun."

His words caused my throat to become thick with emotion and something outside the window became so fascinating it promptly stole my gaze away from Quetz until said emotion diminished and tears no longer threatened to spill. Still, his fingers wove with mine and the song it made my heart sing was a melody I could not ignore.

No matter how I tried.

As Quetz and I trudged up the stairs to our separate bedrooms, his fingers curled around my arm as I opened my door.

"Hey... I have something for you. But if you're too tired, I can give it to you tomorrow..."

I caught myself mirroring one of his crooked smiles, heart fluttering.

Quetz left briefly to fetch the gift from his room as I waited in mine. He returned, folding in behind me I stood in front of the mirror removing my jewellery- few pieces I'd picked up in the Southern Guard to match my dress when I'd bought Graham's birthday gifts.

Quetz's hands were cupped, eyes alight with excitement, as he held something that seemed to be delicate. I turned to face him my gaze drifting from his down to his hands, where a tiny coiled snake sat. It's petite gaze curious.

Quetz's voice was so tender it made something deep within in me purr. "Her name is Nahui."

I studied her in awe. Her eyes were a deep gold and matched her scales: a brilliant mosaic of blues, greens, reds, and golds like Quetz's beast's form. I carefully tasted the syllables. "Nah-hwee?"

He smiled, nodding as he gently took one of my hands in his and turned up my palm. Nahui's tongue flicked out before she unravelled herself. Slithering into my hand and weaving her delicate body around my thumb and forefinger before turning her head towards me as if to see my reaction.

I beamed brightly, a fist of emotion squeezing my heart. Both for her and for Quetz.

My eyes glistened for about the hundredth time tonight.

"Thank you."

Quetz slid his arm around my back and kissed the top of my head. "I thought that you might appreciate having another friend. She's excited to speak with you."

My heart nearly burst with excitement and gratitude.

"She speaks?"

Quetz nodded, his smile broadening at my pleasure and awe.

"She'll have to taste your blood first. But once she does, you'll be able to communicate with her regardless of the distance. She's a descendant of Ouroboros. He was a deity that expressed the unity of all things material and spiritual."

My brow furrowed.

"Was?"

Quetz sighed heavily.

"He was buried somewhere here on Terrenea but he always returns. At some point. Who knows what corner of the dimensions his soul has slithered off to now."

I made a mental note to ask Nahui if she wanted me to find him.

"You should know that she is highly venomous when she wants to be and that she can turn things to gold with her touch. I've only ever seen her do it when she's angry though."

My eyebrows leapt.

"Right. So don't piss her off."

Quetz laughed. "She's quite docile. She's only ever killed one person. Or god, rather."

My jaw dropped. Quetz let out a heavy huff, a look of sadness seeping into his expression.

"Tezcaht. My brother."

My throat worked on a swallow.

"Oh, gods..."

Quetz shook his head as though trying to rid himself of the memory, curls bouncing. "It's a long story that ended with him trying to kill me. Thirst for power, blah, blah, blah." His forefinger curled beneath Nahui's head to gently pet her making a smile illuminate his features once more. "But this magnificent being here saved me."

Nahui nuzzled her head closer against Quetz's finger, and I felt the urge to kiss her in gratitude. How different life would be if Tezcaht had succeeded. And what a precious gift the realms would have been forsaken...

Thankfully, Quetz's voice interrupted my line of thought.

"I imagine you two will get along swimmingly... Oh, and she's also normally much, much larger than this."

I chuckled, narrowing my eyes at him. *Venomous. Enormous. Can turn things to gold with a single touch.*

"Are you actually trying to kill me?"

Quetz gave a belly laugh, Nahui slithered back into his hand and coiled around his wrist before returning to mine.

"I can think of many things I'd love to do to you but I can assure you, killing you isn't one of them."

My breath silently caught, and my core clenched and blossomed with a warmth I tried to mentally slap away.

"It was her idea, to shrink down in size for you. Lest she startle you."

Probably a good idea, I hummed my gratitude toward her.

"You can speak with her too?"

"She's been bonded to me since she hatched. Sank her teeth into me as soon as she did. And she was *much* larger then."

She coiled around my wrist, tongue flicking repeatedly against the pulse point of my wrist.

"She's ready to bond with you, if you are... It is irreversible. She'll become a soul mate of yours. Platonic, of course."

I nodded to her encouragingly. The pupils of her golden eyes widened before she struck, latching onto the inside of my wrist with her fangs. I managed to not wince at the tight burning sensation of her fangs sinking into my flesh. After a moment, I felt as though a slender channel opened in the centre of my chest and connected me directly with her. The channel tingled distinctly and pulled tight as though solidifying before it relaxed and wave of... her being passed through me.

Nahui's fangs retracted and she released me. A tiny droplet of my blood trickling down her neck.

"I see why he's grown so fond of you."

Her voice was deep and smooth. It seemed to wrap and coil around me much like her slender body had done around my wrist as she stared up at me. Quetz's voice filled my mind before I could respond.

"No sharing my secrets, Nahui. That's not fair."

Nahui's tongue flicked towards him and I swore I saw a smile grow on her mouth.

"I'm sure it's nothing she doesn't already know. Or reciprocate," she added pointedly.

My stomach gave a nervous flutter at her words.

"Will you be able to listen in on all of our conversations?"

Quetz gave me a wry smirk.

"Much to my dismay, no. I think she just wants to embarrass me. She does enjoy pushing my buttons."

Nahui's laughter was soft and smooth.

"Not at all, I just know that you need a little encouraging sometimes."

I couldn't help but chuckle in response, and feel a burst of admiration for their close connection. How well they knew each other.

Nahui seemed to read my sentiment.

"Don't worry. You'll have plenty of time to get to know each other if what Quetz-

I felt a sudden tight pull on the tether between Quetz and I as he cut off Nahui's words.

"I'm thoroughly mortified as it is, Nahui. Well done."

Nahui and I both chuckled as she slithered around his hand and up his arm, growing increasingly large as she did. It wasn't until she'd draped herself around his shoulders and arms, looking almost identical to the tattoo I knew lay beneath the dark green matte silk shirt he wore, that she stopped growing.

I studied her, entirely awed by her beauty as the design of her stunning scales grew more discernible.

"Is that your natural size?"

"Not quite."

Nahui slithered off of Quetz's shoulders and onto the bed growing ever larger as she did until her body coiled tightly in the centre of the bed, and was nearly as wide.

My lips parted in awe. Her head was nearly as big as mine.

"Do you mind sharing warmth? Unless you planned on Quetz joining-

"I'd love to share my warmth! With you, I mean. Not Quetz. Unless of course- I mean... I didn't mean-

Nahui chuckled.

"Oh my... How delightful *this is going to be."*

My face blazed its shame. Quetz's eyes seemed to sparkle as he chewed his cheek trying to hide his smile.

I cleared my throat, no longer able to stand my own awkwardness.

"I'm *exhausted.* How about you? Let's go to bed, shall we? I mean- our separate beds. Obviously."

Oh dear gods, what is wrong *with me?*

Quetz, grinning gently all the while, slowly closed the distance between us as though giving me time to stop him. Which, despite all reason, I seemed to powerless to do. He only stopped when our chests grazed. And I was pretty sure the thundering of my heart was audible.

Quetz leaned down towards me. His cheek, slightly rough now from the facial hair he kept shaved away, whispered against mine. The scent of rain, jasmine, and the slightest hint of sandalwood curled around me. He kept his hands stuffed in his pockets as though to prevent himself from doing something... *more.* But eventually, his head turned and his lips gingerly pressed against my cheek. His voice just as tender, and his words for me alone.

"Breathe, Aurelia."

I only managed to resume doing so when he finally stood upright. Our gazes locked.

Quetz's expression held no teasing or mischief. Something far more potent had replaced it.

Neither of us spoke, and the fleeting seconds felt like an eternity of sweet torture. Since the moment I'd laid eyes on him before we'd left for dinner, a warm tingling sensation that throbbed deep inside me had been steadily increasing throughout the entire evening.

By now, if he so much as *breathed* in the direction of my lady bits, I was pretty sure I'd be reduced to a puddle and my last thread of restraint would snap.

And based on the look on his face, he knew it. Thanks to the tether of The Creators' Promise that bound us, he was privy to all my strongest emotions. Sworn and bound to protect me with his life, he was tuned into to me *always*. But just as he could surely feel my impossibly increasing longing for him, he could also feel the warring, lingering weight of my guilt for Kyril, regardless of what he'd done.

I watched Quetz's throat work on a rough swallow as he drew a hand out of his pocket. His thumb caressing my cheek as he leaned in and kissed my forehead.

"Goodnight, Aurelia."

Quetz disappeared, presumably to fold back into his room. The chill that replaced him was enough to bring tears to my eyes. I took a slow, deep breath to steady myself as I turned to face Nahui watching me from the pillow she'd curled up against. Notably, on the side of the bed that was parallel with mine.

Her voice was almost awed.

"Well... That was.... Interesting."

I walked over and flopped onto the bed beside her, groaning loudly into the pillow in response. A moment later I felt the soft, silken warmth of her body slide against mine as though to comfort me. And the gratitude I felt- for her, for Quetz- broke the dam of my tears. I rolled onto my side and curled my body around hers, promising myself to get up and liberate myself of the weight of my stress with a long, hot shower. However, by a power that was not my own, the lights dimmed to nothing and a deep, dreamless sleep swallowed me whole before I could give it a second thought.

TEN

AURELIA

I woke to an empty bed, lifting my head to search for Nahui but found no sign of her other than the rumpled blanket and pillow beside me where she'd slept. Without even having to ask, she responded. *"I was hungry. Just finishing my breakfast."*

I felt a pang of empathy imagining what poor creature had met its end at her fangs. Or constricting body. *"A deer. I make sure they die quickly. I'm not* that *sort of sadist."*

I chose not to dwell on the image. *"Did Darcos or Graham see you yet?"*

"No, I folded to a near by forest."

A pang of relief filled me that she could do such a thing, lest a human mistake her for a threat and do something irreparable.

I felt a gush of warmth and appreciation from her wash over me.

"Don't worry, it would take a lot more than bullets or a knife to kill me."

I felt no small amount of relief at hearing that. Humans were exceedingly volatile creatures, and often *violently* feared the unknown.

"Ok, please be careful."

I felt her being nuzzle against mine affectionately with appreciation before fading away.

Shortly after I'd stepped in the shower, I felt Quetz's presence fold into existence at my bedroom door.

"Quetz?"

His words were a little rushed. Concern lacing them. *"How're you feeling?"*

Anxiety knotted in my stomach, as I quickly rinsed the cleansers from my body. *"Is everything ok?"*

A pause.

"There's been an attack at Nuala's palace."

My heart nearly jumped out of my throat.

"Was she there?"

"Yes. She's... recovering."

I slammed the handle of the shower off and yanked the towel around my body before folding to my bedroom door.

I opened it to find Quetz still standing on the other side of it, his expression pained and radiating an anxiety I'd never seen him with.

My words came out nothing short of panicked. "Can we leave now?" I turned back to my room, rushing to get dressed, as Quetz stepped inside. I let the towel drop to my feet as I pulled on underwear, cursing that I didn't have any fighting silks with me.

"I've already apologized to Darcos and Graham that we had to leave so suddenly."

I turned, yanking a dress over my head, to find Nahui, shrunk, and wrapped around Quetz's forearm. She lifted her head to give me a hiss in admonishment. *"Don't even think about leaving me behind."*

Quetz, Nahui, and I folded into my bedroom of the palace. The feeling of bizarre disbelief and something more morose settled over me. The last time I'd been in this room I'd escaped Pauperes Domos... Quetz my first ally, and spent the first month mourning the death of my brother barely leaving this room... before I'd met Kyril and fallen madly in love. It was less than three months ago. And oh, how my world had changed...

Fear suddenly clenched my heart. For more reasons than one.

"She's in her room?"

Quetz nodded.

"Is Kyril with her?"

A pause. Another nod. I sucked in a sharp breath. I needed to see her but wasn't ready to see him. I began pacing.

"I can... try to distract him. If you prefer."

The gratitude and relief I felt was quickly washed away by the doom. It was an inevitable. I knew I had to confront him eventually. Better to get it over with now, no matter how painful, then to linger with crushing anxiety.

I walked toward my wardrobe and pulled on spare pair of fighting silks that had collected dust there. They were black. Like my mood.

As soon as I slipped them on, as though my fate had been sealed, I turned back to Quetz. My heart pounding so hard I was sure it was trying to escape our fate and the cage of my ribs.

Quetz reached out and gently grasped my arm.

"Breathe, Aurelia... I'm with you. And I won't let him get anywhere near you. Neither will Nahui," who hissed her agreement, "If things get bad, we can just fold back to Darcos'. He can't track us."

"It's not just me I'm worried about," I said, studying the scar on his face.

Finally, his eyes darkened and a small smile of lethal promise curled a corner of his mouth, making me recall the image of Quetz when Kyril had first put the palladium collar on my throat. And I was suddenly less fearful for Quetz, and more so for Kyril.

I took a deep steadying breath and felt Quetz push a wave of calm and support over me, as did Nahui as she slithered up to my shoulder and draped herself around me like a necklace. A little of my trepidation eased as my heart swelled with gratitude.

As soon as we folded into Nuala's room, my heart gave another traitorous leap in my chest as though it were trying to abandon me. The form of Kyril's dark silhouette stood over Nuala who laid, whether rendered unconscious, or simply asleep I had no idea. But I'd already reached out to her spirit the moment Quetz had given me the news, and felt that her life force was still strong.

Kyril turned sharply to face us. His face fell before contorting with anguish at the sight of me before folding directly in front of me. Or Quetz, rather, who had presumably predicted the move, and placed himself in front of me.

Kyril growled a warning.

"Don't make an enemy of me, Quetzacoatl."

Quetz's response came out with alarming calm.

"You've already made yourself one of mine."

The heat of Kyril's blossoming anger radiated off of him. I stepped around Quetz, Nahui having disappeared to god's knew where. I cursed inwardly as my voice came out a tremble despite my best efforts.

"Kyril..."

"My fire-

The words made me seethe as my rage blossomed anew.

"Don't you *dare* call me that."

Kyril's face fell, all signs of fury gone to be replaced with hurt. A grim flicker of understanding further darkening his burning ember gaze.

"Aurelia... I understand why you may hate me now but perhaps if I had let you kill me and then live without me for two hundred years you'd understand."

"Where is Caelus?"

"I don't know... Where are the sigillums?"

My jaw clenched so hard it ached. I stepped around him, followed by Quetz, and strode towards Nuala's beside, feeling a bit more relief with each step. She looked... Ok. No scars, or other signs of wounds.

"What happened?"

Kyril reappeared, folding beside me, his expression grim.

"We'd come to prepare ourselves against Caelus' retaliation. Early this morning a group of rebel fae from..."

My throat felt like it was trying to swallow a sandy boulder of dread.

"The rebel fae from Pauperes Domos... They'd somehow snuck into the castle. She alerted her guards but by the time they'd arrived she was already unconscious. Although three of the rebels were dead, one survived. He's in the dungeon."

"Have you gotten anything out of them?"

"Only that they have more attacks planned."

"Did he tell you how to heal her and make her wake up?"

"... No."

"Take me to him."

Quetz and Kyril stood beside me as I stared down at the sagging form of a bloodied, burned, and unconscious fae. I diligently ignored the hammering wound in my chest, recalling the last set of circumstances in which I'd stood between the same two males in this very dungeon.

Kyril and I had just freed Quetz who'd then happily chosen to bind himself to me. The time before that was when I'd just escaped

Paupers Domos, Quetz and I both prisoners- me for a night, and him for those 33 years.

Through his own magic, he'd consoled me by bringing me, in an astral projection of some kind, to my murdered brother's soul...

Before I'd ever been able to reconnect with my powers and my past life's memories that I'd been shut off too, thanks to Caelus, my entire life. Until Morwen had been able to *forcefully* remove his binding.

Quetz had brought my otherwise inconsolable spirit peace. I sent a silent prayer up to my brother whose contented spirit I could now feel, though we couldn't communicate. My powers only enabled me to guide spirits by 'suggestion' or force. I couldn't directly speak with them once they were in the dimensions beyond.

And as for the fae male currently suspended by magic suppressing manacles in the middle of the room- his life force was definitely waning. His spirit a mere whisper. He wasn't even conscious, and I knew there was no way I'd be able to get him to talk like this.

I stepped forward, laying my hand on his shoulder, willing my energy to course forth and heal him. After a few moments, he slowly picked his head up, piercing blue eyes meeting mine. Images of the recent past filling my mind. I had seen that gaze. When that first battle had broken out in Pauperes Domos and the masked rebels had attacked us, many of them escaping. And again, I had seen that familiar shock of pale cerulean eyes looming in the crowds at this past summer solstice celebration. Another stab of guilt found me. He had gotten away, both times because of me.

· · ·

"The traitor," he seethed.

My stomach twisted into a heinous knot of guilt, remorse, and fury. A great many of the reasons that caused it had nothing to do with him. I heard Nahui voice my own gut response. *"Promise me you'll kill him, please."* Despite her words, her voice soothed my anger. Even though I knew couldn't make that promise. *"Where are you?"*

"Searching your nexus' room. Among a few other things... I'll know if you need me."

The rebel fae laughed grossly in disgust, drawing me back to the room. "Can't even deny it, can you?"

My words came out a growl. "Tell me how to heal her, and I swear to let you leave this dungeon alive."

The fae's features contorted into a sneer, eyes shifting between the three of us.

"You can't heal her. She's doomed."

Quetz's inhuman snarl behind me made the hairs on the back of my neck rise. "You lie."

The fae spat a wad of blood at my feet. "She's cursed. There's nothing to heal. You have to break the curse."

My hand shot out and lifted him off the ground by the throat. The action only made him grin revealing unusually long, sharp canines.

"Your next words either tell me exactly how to *remedy* this situation or you die here. And I'll make certain your soul seeks eternity in a hell realm."

I tugged on his life force and finally his eyes widened in fear, his skin paling by several shades, as he croaked his submission.

He coughed violently as his windpipe resumed its normal shape. "You have until the next new moon. As the moon fades, so will she. And there's nothing you, *or your powers,* can do about it unless you feel like sacrificing yourself."

"Speak plainly," Kyril growled beside me.

The fae chuckled, a smug scowl creeping across his face.

"I did. Your traitor whore has to die if you want your *Queen* back."

Kyril's fist hit him so hard I heard bones crack. The fae sagged unconscious again.

My gaze slid to Kyril's, words clipped.

"You're making this take longer than necessary."

My skin crawled as I grasped his sweaty, bloody head with my hand and healed his concussion so he'd wake. I did *not*, however, heal his broken cheekbone and nose.

The fae's groan turned into a snarl as he woke up in what I'm sure was absolute agony.

"Explain."

He spat blood again, this time narrowly missing Kyril's boot.

"It's an *anima libera* curse. A *soul trade.* The curse is broken when you *willingly* exchange your life for hers. But being the traitor that you are, we both know you're not capable of heroism."

I narrowed my eyes at him, wilfully ignoring the guillotine that was now hanging over my head.

"I *freed* you from the slums of Pauperes Domos. What have I ever done but help you?"

His words turned to venom.

"You fought along side the same Queen who killed your ancestors, You slaughtered the very people you suffered and bled alongside slaving away in the quarry. Your parents are *dead* because of her and The Lord of the Northern Guard- *The Queen's Right Hand. The Burning Warrior.* And yet you eagerly spread your legs for him-"

The fae's words cut off in a strangled cry as Quetz shifted into his incorporeal form- brilliant gold, silver, and black whorls of pure magic, and something that I didn't yet recognize or understand- everything in the dungeon began to shake and vibrate and draw towards him.

The rebel fae's voice came out a shriek.

"You can't kill me! I told you how to break the curse! She swore to let me leave the dungeon alive!"

Quetz's voice was a harbinger of doom.

"I made no such promise."

"There are more attacks planned-

"I know. You've already shown me all I needed."

The white's of the rebel fae's eyes grew wider as even the pebbles and dirt on the floor shook and rose towards him as if he were some vortex of gravity, pulling in all forms of energy and matter towards himself. And as it did, his form increased in size.

The winds rose and spun around us like a hurricane, though there was no window from which they could have come. His form became so bright I had to squint my eyes.

I looked down to see even my hair being pulled towards him.

Kyril's arm wrapped around my waist, pulling me against him.

I couldn't help but recoil. Mostly in fear that he would do something like slap another palladium collar around my neck and fold out of the dungeon with me while Quetz was distracted.

I shoved him away and stepped closer to Quetz. The hurt in Kyril's eyes burned me to the core. Unable to bare it, I shifted my attention back to Quetz whose magic, ether, and essence formed an even larger shadow of his corporeal arm.

He reached out and grasped the fae's head whose eyes's rolled in the back as he sagged in Quetz's grip. The fae's jaw slackened wide, releasing some pained animalistic noise.

I stepped closer, turning to look at Quetz. The only part that I could recognise was the inhuman glow of his brilliant turquoise eyes beaming like twin alien suns amidst the whorls of his magic and ether. I felt his magic and essence pulling me, drawing me in.

Distantly, I could hear Kyril's voice shout for me.

My lips parted in awe.

I knew that if I had any sense whatsoever, I would be afraid. I *should* be afraid. Even though he was sworn to protect me, his power was so formidable and... beyond anything I'd ever witnessed. A normal, healthy reaction should be awe-some fear. But the only part of that I felt was simply awe.

As if reading my mind Quetz's words filled my mind.

"You are not afraid?"

"No... Should I be?"

"Never."

All at once, Quetz's incorporeal form collapsed in on itself like a dying star and all the remained was his corporal form. Naked. Again.

We were really going to have to do something about this. My face was still gaping in awe at him, inspiring him to gift me with one of his mischievous smiles as he parroted my earlier words back to me.

"I didn't realize my nudity caused you so much discomfort."

I chuckled a soft laugh, parroting the response he'd then given me before I could think better of it.

"Discomfort is hardly the word I would use to describe what your nudity does to me."

Quetz erupted with laughter and as he stepped forward, his breathtaking 'god-uniform' covering his nudity. He returned to my side, the now dead fae revealed. Or what was left of him. A few ashes drifting to the dungeon floor. Not even the manacles remained.

I whistled loudly, trying to ignore the panic and anxiety I felt returning at the ceaseless echo of the dead rebel fae's words. '... *The curse is broken when you willingly exchange your life for hers...*'

As though determined to ruin my efforts, Kyril vocalized my greatest fear, and the stare he was giving Quetz was downright lethal.

"The new moon rises in two days. Whatever your decision, we need those sigillums."

I didn't move from Quetz's side as I drew Kyril's gaze back to mine, pain replacing fury.

"There is no longer any 'we' when it comes to the sigillums, Kyril."

The embers of his eyes burned but his voice remained restrained.

"You and I need to have a conversation in private."

I huffed a mirthless laugh.

"The only way I'm doing that, is if you put a palladium collar around *your* neck."

His jaw feathered and I knew it was guilt that dampened the fire that I could see burning within him.

And in that moment, despite how much pain it caused me... I couldn't bring myself to console him.

"I'm getting the fuck out of this dungeon."

ELEVEN

AURELIA

T folded back to the beach at Darcos'. A few moments later Quetz appeared beside me. Tears swelled in my eyes, and my voice came out a croak.

"I'd like to visit her again. When Kyril isn't there."

Quetz's only response was a nod.

"Do you know much about the anima libera?"

"He wasn't lying but we can go to Nuala's palace library, or any another you prefer... Perhaps Morwen knows of something."

Fear twisted my heart, it's claws sinking in deep. I turned to meet his gaze, having to crane my neck because we stood so close. Tears swelled in my eyes as my words trembled. "I won't let her die for me. This is my fault. If I hadn't..." My voice cracked and I had to bite my cheek *hard* to suppress the choked sob that threatened to escape.

Quetz's long, strong arms wrapped around me as he spoke.

"Aurelia, we will find a way. Together. I've seen it."

My breath caught, hope renewed.

"How?"

"I have to scry and sift through the potentialities more. But there is a way. I know what I've seen. Even Nuala's seen it. She saw a near, and distant, future where *she* lived. And *you* were there. We both saw it... I *will* find a way for you *both* to live."

Quetz's voice cracked and I looked up to find the evidence of his emotion swelling in his eyes. Normally so sure and unwavering in his confidence. His nonchalance. His lightheartedness and joviality.

My heart bloomed with something that didn't entirely extinguish my fear but *eclipsed* it and flooded me with courage.

And before I could think better of it, I stood on the tips of my toes, wove my arms around his neck, and pulled his mouth against mine in a bruising kiss. Every atom in my body erupted and overflowed with an emotion that I had been desperately trying to push away and ignore for longer than I could bare to admit. Our lips slid against one another in a passionate caress as we both groaned in a way that vocalized both our pain and pleasure.

He leaned further into me, his arms enveloping my waist and picking me up to pull me against his chest. Feet off the ground, my legs twined around his waist as he braced his arms beneath my bum and thighs. His hands gripping my flesh in a way that curled heat deep within me. I folded us into my bedroom, and without missing a beat he laid me down on the bed.

My core clenched with need and despair as the *enormous* evidence of his desire was now pressed against my stomach- and reached beyond my belly button. His tongue licked the seam of my mouth, making my heart leap at the silent request.

I opened for him eagerly, my tongue meeting his for the first time in a dance that was gradually shifting from rough and passionate to something tender.

With every stroke and caress of his tongue I swore I could feel it against my clit.

A soft, high pitched moan escaped me and in response he growled his satisfaction. My hands roamed across the muscled plains, peaks, and valleys of his herculean body as his own hands explored all the soft dips and curves of mine- steadily approaching the rounded peaks of my breasts. His hand slid up the inside of my top, thumbs caressing the underside of my breasts.

I sucked his bottom lip into my mouth and bit it gently, pulling back slightly to meet his heavy lidded gaze. When I realized he was still wearing his god-uniform, I released it. And couldn't suppress the grin that split my face at the sight of his large feathered headdress.

"You really do look breathtaking in this outfit... Though you're no less breathtaking without it."

His gaze softened, brows furrowing softly.

"Aurelia... From the moment I saw you..."

I huffed a sad laugh. "In the dungeons?"

His brow furrowed deeper, shaking his head.

"No... Long before that..."

My throat worked on a rough swallow thinking of all the past held.

How Quetz and I had ended up in that dungeon.

I tried to will the stab of pain at the thought of Kyril away. My voice came out a whisper.

"I can't think about all that right now..."

Quetz opened his mouth to say something but then closed it in an effort to respect my wishes.

Weaving my fingers through the silky curls of his hair, I gently pressed my lips to the corner of his mouth and slowly kissed, licked, and nipped my way across his jaw until I reached his ear.

"Thank you, Quetz... I... There's so much you've done for me and if we do get through this... Regardless of what happens between us, I'd be honored if you allowed me to spend the rest of our days together, however long or brief, proving to you just how grateful I am..."

Quetz shifted to meet my gaze, stroking the apple of my cheek with his thumb.

"Aurelia... You're the most important thing to me- in this world and all the worlds beyond. If I have to die with you just to bring your soul back with me, I will...," A mischievous grin tilted his lips as he continued, "And as *delicious* as it sounds, you never need to *prove* anything to me. I will continue to spend my days protecting you and being there for you so long as you'll have me, regardless."

I searched his gaze finding what I knew I would: the same emotion I'd always had for him from the night I'd met him: when after willingly being trapped in that mirror in Nuala's dungeon to help me, he'd befriended me, and brought me to that distant realm in a dimension far beyond our own to see my brother after he'd just died at my side.

But I knew that before I could move forward with this... towards anything beyond whatever *this* was, as complicated as it had already become... I knew that we needed to take care of Nuala first. And I had to... deal with Kyril.

As always, Quetz knew where my thoughts had wandered. He leaned forward and kissed my forehead before pressing one last lingering kiss to my lips that made my heart swell before he shifted to lay beside me on the bed and tucked me against him.

I felt the fighting silks leave my body leaving me in my underwear, tucked beneath the blankets of my bed. The warmth of his now naked body, save for what felt like silk boxers, curled against mine with his arm wrapped around my waist and legs woven with mine.

My bedroom light dimmed into nothing as he spoke softly, lips grazing my shoulder as he held me to him.

"Do you remember the promise I made you? When you freed me from the mirror in the dungeon?"

Emotion swelled in me again that had me smiling to myself. Rogue tears spilling onto my pillow as I recalled the memory.

"Yes."

He began to repeat it softly as though he were reciting its words with new found love and appreciation.

"By the power of The Creators, The Many and The One...The Ones, all things benevolent to which all paths lead... including the teachers of suffering and all that is deemed malicious; that holds all the nine realms

and beyond in balance with the infinite divine... the unifying source that is beyond mortal and immortal comprehension, all for the evolution and betterment of all creation... that I, Quetzacoatl, The Creator God, and Eternal Guardian of Time, Wind and Rain, The Arts, and All Good Things..."

With each word he spoke aloud, emotion I knew I couldn't yet vocalize filled my chest to bursting. I twisted in his arms and turned to face him, nuzzling my face into his chest as a seemingly endless river of tears spilled down my cheeks. The wind of an unknown breeze stirred gently in the room, caressing what remained exposed of my face, neck, and shoulders as he stroked my hair with his hand.

"I am the feathered-serpent; One of the four sons of Ometeotl the God of Life and Duality. I bind my soul to the will of Aurelia Eleftheran and her eternal form until she wills an end to my solemn vow."

He pressed a kiss to my forehead, tears still spilling, and as my eyes slipped shut I drifted into another deep, dreamless sleep.

TWELVE

AURELIA

"We're going to need Morwen."

The watery moonlight of the waning crescent trickled into the bedroom, illuminating Quetz's silhouette as he stood in front of the window staring out at the dark horizon of the tumultuous sea. The winds rattled the windows and shutters of the house and I had to wonder if it was a reflection of Quetz's mood. Probably, considering it was one his domains.

When I didn't respond, he turned to me, eyes glowing faintly. Despite having only slept a handful of hours, I somehow still felt rested, and energized as I rose from the bed.

"Let's go."

Morwen already stood waiting at the gates of Bataan's castle when we arrived. We hadn't told her we were coming, assuming she'd have been asleep, but she had an uncanny way of predicting and *knowing* things that even I, as a goddess, possessed no natural way of discovering.

. . .

The flickering flames of the torches mounted on the walls illuminated her long silvery har. At 6 feet tall, with her lithe athletic figure, she dwarved even a few of the castle guards who seemed entirely unsurprised by our arrival when we folded only a few feet in front of them. Morwen pushed off the massive stone door she was leaning against. It had carved reliefs of tremendous snarling wolves with Batlaan himself, who was a Lykanthir, endowing him with the ability to shift into an enormous wolf.

She gave us a dramatic yawn before turning to lead us into the castle.

"Took you long enough."

As Quetz and I began to follow her, a seven foot tall shadow peeled itself from the wall to follow us.

Nox.

His dark stoney blue skin and black attire blended with the darkness effortlessly. He had a voice to match- like smoothest whiskey and glass shards. Rough and menacing with an air of aristocracy. Being The Elven Prince of Tenebris Dryadlis- the dark elven realm- after all.

"Good to see you... Free. Aurelia... Quetz."

He bowed slightly before stepping into stride beside us. Between he and Quetz, who stood around 6 and a half feet, and was also broader than Nox was, both had to slow their steps so I could keep up without breaking into a jog. And my pace, lest they fall asleep waiting, was brisk at the very least.

"Always a pleasure...," Quetz spoke for the both of us.

I felt slightly at a loss for words. The last time I'd seen him Kyril had tried to kidnap me.

Which he had clearly been waiting to bring up.

"How's Kyril?"

I couldn't help the frown that carved my face.

Quetz, thankfully, rescued me again from having to respond.

"Unhinged, I imagine. But he no longer has any of the sigillums, and they're safely hidden somewhere far beyond his grasp. So we've got that going for us."

Nox chuckled even as sadness settled on his features. His gaze briefly fell to mine.

I gulped, swallowing all the pain and anger to keep myself steady.

A familiar cool press of flesh draped itself around my neck and although she didn't speak, Nahui's energy curled against me in an embrace.

Nox's eyes widened in curiosity.

"Hello," he purred.

I glanced to find Nahui's head rising from my shoulder, tongue flicking.

"This is Nahui. Nahui. Nox."

"It's an honor... "

Nahui held his gaze for a few moments before returning her head to my shoulder.

"I smell my grandfather on him. Faintly..."

"Would you like me to ask about him?"

"... Another time, perhaps."

"What did you discover at the palace?"

"Your nexus is..."

An all too familiar presence, an all too familiar heat pressed onto my magic behind me making all my hairs stand on end and anxiety to sinks its claws into my gut.

"Here," I finished for her flatly, though I was still curious as to what she was going to say but...

Despite my better judgement, I found myself stopping in my tracks to look at him. Quetz had warned me that he would end up here. Though we weren't sure how.

Morwen gave me a compassionate glance back, hesitating in front of the castle of stone, wood, and stained glass.

"We'll be in the study waiting whenever you're ready. You're welcome to wait with us, Quetz. He won't be able to fold in or out of the castle so you don't have to worry about anyone being *kidnapped*."

Nox joined her side, flashing Kyril a look of wounded displeasure, as he took her hand in his before folding out of sight.

Kyril's hardened gaze slammed into mine and I couldn't help the scowl that marred my face in response.

Who had told him we were here? We'd just arrived.

Quetz, in order to hide us, had cloaked our magic and 'energetic signatures'. And I had temporarily silenced the tether between us so I couldn't feel his emotions, nor he mine. I'd also constructed a mental and magical barrier to keep him from reading my thoughts, or from being able to intrusively speak to me mind-to-mind. So although I couldn't actually *feel* Kyril's fury, it was readable in-person none-theless. And I'd hoped that having braced myself, my reaction to seeing him wouldn't be so visceral. Or painful.

My hope was wholly misplaced. Immediately, my stomach twisted into vicious knots. Every atom in my body revolted feeling like a damning wall was pressing in on me until I was crushed beneath its will.

But instead of it being directed at me, his gaze shifted to Quetz. "*Quetzacoatl.*"

Damn it.

I took a step in front of Quetz to block him.

"Get out of the way, Aurelia."

Nahui hissed her displeasure at him, growing in size around my shoulders. Kyril stepped back, surprise briefly disrupting his hard-ened glare.

Quetz folded behind Kyril, directing his attention back to himself.

I folded into the space beside them, ready to dive between them if I had to.

Kyril's words came out a snarl.

"*Undo it. Now.*"

Genuine sadness and empathy seeped into Quetz's expression.

"I won't do anything to jeopardize her safety. Even if it means helping her hide from you until you come to your senses."

A vein on Kyril's forehead throbbed its warning.

"She's my *nexus mate*. I'm the only one she's safe with."

A growl leapt up my throat and spat the words.

"You deceived me. You lied. You betrayed your closest friends and allies. *Your* ally kidnapped and nearly murdered me. *You* tried to kidnap me. You put a fucking palladium collar around my neck. You threaten to destroy the world in which we live. And then when I tried to stop you, you tried to *burn* me and Quetz, despite our shared histories together."

Kyril's pain radiated from him in hot waves.

"I know that it's hard to understand this now but I'm doing all of this to protect you."

I shook my head in disbelief, my words bitter.

"You're doing this to protect *yourself.*"

Kyril held my gaze, anguish permeating his features before hardening again with his resolution.

"One day you'll understand. And if you have to hate me until then, so be it." His gaze returned to Quetz.

"Lift your magic from our bond before this ends in bloodshed."

I gasped my shock, fury burning my veins.

Nahui slithered off me as she grew to her full size, raising her head until she towered above Kyril and hissed viciously. Kyril's sword manifested in his hand only for Quetz to roll his eyes and with a wave of his hand, she disappeared.

Nahui scowled her reproach in our minds.

"You fucking asshole."

When Kyril returned his focus, Quetz only heaved a sad sigh despite the furious battle-hardened warrior threatening him. Kyril had proven to be an exceptional warrior over the centuries, having helped Nuala win the war despite being so greatly outnumbered and overpowered. If Kyril had been threatening anyone else, other than Quetz, I would have been terrified for them. And although I didn't yet have any idea as to how much experience he had in waging war... There was no doubt in my mind that if there was anyone who would walk away from this fight, it would be Quetz.

Before Quetz could respond I stepped between them, practically snarling. "Don't you *dare* threaten him. And he wasn't the one who silenced our bond. I did."

Kyril's sword vanished as his jaw dropped, eyes slamming into mine. "*Why?* How could you do such a thing?"

I could feel the heat of the guard's gazes on us and willed a barrier around us, including one that prevented Quetz from hearing. I sent a silent apology to him and promised to explain later. I didn't want to add salt to Kyril's wound, or fuel to the burgeoning flames of his ire.

"You've broken my trust, Kyril. The damage inflicted by your actions are beyond repair. Yet you remain remorseless. Why wouldn't I silence it, if for no other reason than to give myself a modicum of peace?"

Kyril's jaw flexed repeatedly, the corners of his mouth turning down.

"I knew you'd be angry, and yes, hurt, when you found out but I thought you would at least be able to appreciate and recognize everything I'm *sacrificing*. For *you*."

I huffed a mirthless laugh in disbelief even as furious tears forced their way to my eyes.

"I see exactly what you're sacrificing, and it is *killing* me, Kyril. But if you really believe that you're doing this for anyone but your-self, you're delusional, and far worse off than I had imagined."

He shook his head at me, giving me a piteous look laced with disgust.

"I would never wish upon you everything I went through after I returned from that battlefield to find your headless corpse with its heart burned out after Caelus murdered you. *In your sleep.* Nor would I wish the ensuing 200 years of suffering and grief on you. Or watching your mother be murdered in front of your eyes. And countless other loved ones... But I thought you would at least find it within yourself to empathize with me. And I never in a million years would have imagined you would be this selfish and judgemental, Aurelia."

The words hit me like a slap, indignant fury sinking its claws into me and yanking those heinous tears over my cheeks.

"I imagine your suffering was beyond soul-crushing, and for that I am sorry. But you seem to have forgotten that you're not the only one here who has lost loved ones, or even nexus mates. Yet you are the only one who seems more than willing to become the harbinger of that suffering to anyone who stands in your way. And not just anyone, but *everyone,* if necessary."

Kyril's indignance mirrored my own as he ground out his words.

"I would fight with my life to protect them from such a thing happening. Aeternia has known two hundred years of peace but as you and I are both learning- *nothing ever lasts.* As we speak, rebel fae plot against us. And who knows what war they may bring to our doorstep. It only strengthens my resolve to open this doorway. *Somehow,* they made it into Nuala's palace. *No one* is untouchable.

Can't you see that? At least if we were to open that doorway, we wouldn't have to fear the death of our loved ones. I wouldn't have to fear the death of *you.* No matter who or what came through that doorway, we would always find our way back to each other without having to wait centuries, or millennia, or eons to do it."

The tether between us, despite my magic silencing our connection, burned furiously. I could see clearly Kyril's warped logic and justification for his actions.

But he had no idea the true gravitas of the consequences of opening that doorway, and nor did I. Neither of us had been here the first time but based on what Quetz had witnessed, it seemed we were fortunate that it was only these mysterious 'godly' beings who'd come through it. Perhaps the next time we wouldn't be so lucky. If that door opened again, perhaps Aeternia would become a wasteland, or worse, a hell realm.

The distance between us eroded even further and I felt as though I'd been impaled on a fiery hot poker as it's wielder twisted it in a vengeful stab that reached my soul. I felt something between us give way. Like a bridge, burning, and leaving only a yawning chasm in its wake.

"I understand your logic, Kyril but you have no idea the true potential for apocalypse that opening those doorways could bring, like swiftly and violently ushering us all into an era of a sunless dawn where *nothing* remains. And I won't pretend to know what it feels like to watch my nexus die but I do know that I would never risk such a thing or hurt you, or anyone I love, to spare myself suffering. And that you know just as well as I do, you wouldn't hesitate to do just that to save yourself the loss if you could have."

Kyril's expression only hardened as his misery worked its way through him.

"Yes, I would. Without hesitation."

Tears, in an a ceaseless deluge, abandoned the dams of my eyelids as I felt something tangible between us snap and give way.

"Then I fear there is nothing left for us to salvage between us."

I dropped the barrier to see Quetz still waiting for me, thankfully. Kyril's words hit me like a bad omen as I turned away from him.

"One day you'll change your mind, Aurelia. You'll see."

I no longer had the strength to respond. As I turned on my heel to leave, Kyril's hand shot out but before it could reach me Quetz folded into the space in front of me, causing Kyril to grab Quetz's arm instead. Kyril jerked his hand away, growling as if he'd been burned.

The grin that split Quetz's face was nothing short of malefic. *"Don't* touch her. Unless you *want* this to 'end in bloodshed'."

Miraculously the three of us made it into Batlaan's castle without spilling any blood. We'd folded individually into her study, if that's what it could be called considering it looked more like a laboratory, greenhouse, and museum all rolled up into one stained glass lounge. She stood in front of Nox drinking a glass of amber liquid as he sat on a chaise longue in front of her. She seemed awfully relaxed about all of this. Instead of reassuring me, it only further unnerved me.

"Your things are still in the guest room, by the way ... And if you'd like a place to stay, where Kyril *can't* reach you," she said flicking her eyes at him pointedly, "Our doors are always open, darling,"

Kyril stared daggers at her but his previous ire, after our conversation, had seemed to have strongly waned. My heart was genuinely on the precipice of self-annihilation. And being here in this castle only made it all the worse. The last time we had been here, less than a week ago, I'd still been living in blithely ignorant bliss thinking Kyril wasn't scheming behind our backs. We'd still been madly in love. Our nexus bond stronger than ever. Or so I'd thought. And now it had been all but incinerated.

I didn't know whether or not a nexus bond could actually do such a thing... But it had definitely 'snapped' into place and come alive when we had first bonded in this lifetime. By having sex. As though our coupling had given water to a seed that had then blossomed and bloomed into the visceral tether joining us at the spirit.

I frowned at her words. Somehow he had known we would be here and had been able to get in.

"Who told him I would be here?"

Morwen threw me an apologetic glance.

"I did."

My jaw dropped, eyes leaping between the two of them.

"What?!"

"Because you might need his help."

I ground my teeth so hard I was surprised I didn't crack molar.

"Ya know... At this point, death is looking rather promising," I grumbled.

Morwen threw her head back and laughed.

"That's the spirit."

THIRTEEN

AURELIA

"Time there will be different. What is one minute here, could feel like hours there. Or days... Years, even. Or vice, versa. And there's no way of knowing what to expect. Other than the answer to your question lies on the other side. Which could appear in the form of a person, a test, a song, a memory, a vision... a lifetime. I wish I could give you more guidance but... Be assured that if two days pass here, before the new moon rises, Kyril will come find you and bring you back."

Morwen's words brought me *zero* comfort. In fact, they did the opposite and I was about ready to just go back to Nuala's, pull my own soul from my body, and just hope for the best.

The group of us stood around a large silver basin the size of a large bathtub that sat on a dais and was filled with a liquid so black it absorbed all the light around us. Although the surface was completely still, filled precisely to the brim, and looking ready to spill over- it gave no reflection. I stared down at it, my unease nearly as powerful as the magic pouring off of it in thundering waves that hummed and vibrated a deep, monotone, oscillating melody against my skin. The energy felt neither good, or bad. Just powerful. And indifferent, which was perhaps the most unsettling part. Indifference when wielding power promised mercilessness, and meant that whatever I walked, or swam, into on the other side of that liquid... Nothing and no one would save me, and I would be forced to endure my worst nightmares if that's what it chose to show me.

Morwen slipped a reassuring hand over my shoulder and Nahui- despite me not having introduced them- nuzzled her head against her hand as Morwen gave her a loving look before she returned her gaze to me.

"Don't worry about holding your breath."

My throat worked roughly on a swallow as she continued, my heart hammering in my chest. Not wanting to cause anymore pain or animosity, I responded to her mind-to-mind.

"Can't Nahui and Quetz come with me?"

Her expression alone gave a clear answer but she responded anyway.

"They could, but you'd all end up in different times and places. Even if you ask the same question... You'll only see what you need to see. And only a nexus mate can find you on the other side if you get lost."

She paused, studying my expression before continuing aloud.

"Listen, whatever happens on the other side... you will come back but you might be a different person and you need to mentally prepare yourself for that. And remember, that we *will* pull you out if we need to."

I was tempted to ask what her experiences were like but we were incredibly short on time, and I was also mildly terrified of her answers.

Quetz stood beside me, his fingers discreetly grazing mine in reassurance and support. Thankfully, the action was shielded by the bathtub, or I'm pretty sure Kyril would have attempted murder. When I looked up at him, the pain tightening his face made my heart clench in empathy.

"I wish it were you that would come to get me," I whispered to Quetz mind-to-mind.

And it was true. I didn't trust Kyril anymore. I didn't know if I ever could. And I was still deeply wounded by him. His selfish actions had shown me that when it came down to it... he was only really protecting himself.

But I did trust Quetz.

I found my gaze pulled across from me to Kyril who stood beside Nox on the other side of the basin. His features were pulled tight with anxiety, eyes burning a quiet fire. Nahui slid onto Quetz's shoulders as I gave his hand one last squeeze before climbing up the steps of the dais. I looked down into the surface of the tar black liquid that only stared back like an abysmal chasm.

I dipped an exploratory hand in the inky liquid. The surface of the liquid remained still, not a ripple in sight. And though my hand scooped up a small palmful, when I let it spill between my fingers, my hand remained dry. Heart thundering in my ears, I gave one last look over my shoulder at Quetz.

"Nexus or not, Aurelia... If you need me, I will find you. Whether in this dimension or the next."

My heart swelled, soothing the fear gripping it as his words gave me pause. Kyril had once given me a similar promise... But whereas Kyril would protect me and rescue me to the ends of the worlds, and literally burn the worlds down for me... I know knew that he was doing it more for himself than anyone else. So that he wouldn't have to suffer an existence without me because of what I gave and had to offer him as his nexus. When push came to shove, it wasn't about me or my wellbeing.

Quetz, on the other hand, would protect me and rescue me, and go to the ends of worlds for me, not for his own well being but for mine. It was selfless.

Tears swelled in my eyes as the realization hit me and I only felt sorry that it had taken me this long to realize it. Gaze still lingering on him as I hesitated at the edge of the basin, my words gave me newfound purpose and courage.

"Nexus or not, Quetzacoatl, I love you."

And then I dove headfirst into the chasm of the unknown.

FOURTEEN

QUETZACOATL

Morwen and Nox had gone to bed. Kyril was... The Creators knew where, and I didn't even particularly care at this point. And Batlaan and Eleni were both still in Lux Dryadalis dealing with the aftermath of Eleni's father dying- or having been killed, rather, thanks to Aurelia- and now having to take the reigns as Empress of Lux Dryadilis. A task she seemed to have no desire in undertaking.

In any case, I was grateful for the time alone. I needed to scry. I needed to be prepared for when Aurelia came back. How she could safely move forward with everything- from sacrificing herself to save Nuala, to making it back to her body and our realms safely, keeping those sigillums out of Kyril's hands even if we needed to use them to get her back and then promptly close them... if that was even possible... And how she could move forward with Kyril, her nexus mate, if that was what she wanted... As much as it fucking killed me to imagine.

Finding these answers were the only way to even remotely soothe the tremendous anxiety that I had threatening to burst from my skin. Literally. I could feel my winged-serpent form bursting at the seems, wanting to take over. To protect, to fight and destroy. To fuck. Something to burn off this fear for Aurelia and whatever she was having to go through on the other side of Morwen's portal, and whatever she would soon have to go through on this side of it.

But I had no desire to do any of those things. Well... except for the latter, if Aurelia would one day have me. I wasn't going to get my hopes up. I hadn't peeked into those potentialities yet because... well... it felt unfair to have that kind of knowledge or advantage over her. If I knew how to make things work out to my advantage, it would be nothing less than manipulative to make those play out. And, ultimately, Kyril was her nexus. That was a bond I would never dare to meddle with. Even though Kyril had seemingly lost his mind somewhere along the way, and she deserved far better than what he had done. Was doing. And although I couldn't fathom the pain of seeing the desecrated corpse of my nexus- the other half of my soul- I could fathom having to live for two hundred years without them... Because I'd already done it. For eons. I also couldn't imagine doing something that was against their will, and hurting them, to prevent my own suffering.

I shook my head, as though the action would make the hurricane of thoughts in my mind calm, sliding down the wall to sit on the floor across from the Waters of Kismet that Aurelia dove into a few minutes ago. With every breath I took, I sat on edge, half-expecting her to climb back out of them.

Linear time as we experienced it in this dimension was little more than an illusion. And just as Morwen had explained, what was one minute here, could be eons there.

Or vice versa.

It all depended on what she needed to be shown. Long before the Waters of Kismet had ever come into Morwen's possession, I'd once met a being... whose origin went too far back for me dare to venture and had no name that he could remember... that had gone through the portal of those waters and experienced the birth and death of an entire planet...

When he'd come back, only seven minutes had past. His wife and children had stood there waiting for him but when he returned, he didn't even recognise them and was barely a shadow of himself.

Focus.

I rested my head against the wall and forced my breathing to become slow, deep, and steady as I reached out with an extension of my spirit to the vastness of the verses for that singular thread that connected me to all of time, space, and all that lay beyond.

It was a sensation similar to someone sticking their hand out into an abyss and waiting to feel something, or someone, reach back and pull you in. To put it reductively. And when they did, they became a part of you. And just as you became a part of them, they became a part of... everything.

As I reached that thread, a multidimensional map- far more than merely the three or four dimensions we could fathom- lit up like some ever moving, shifting, morphing, whirling vortex of a neural network that was impossible to traverse by fives senses alone. In order to navigate it, it required you to use something akin to intuition, but truly so much more and trying to describe it was like trying to fit the ocean in a handbag.

A handbag obviously not even being the proper vessel to try and hold any amount of liquid. But here we are. Bound by three dimensions. Or well, four dimensions, for me.

I willed my spirit to Aurelia's, consciously blocking out aspects that pertained to our relationship- whatever it was- and focused on what would be the very near future for her. Specifically, what would happen directly after she returned and how we could get her spirit safely back to it's body after she abandoned it to exchange her life for Nuala's. I had visited these potentialities before but, I needed more than just a general idea of how things could play out. I needed to know how to find her spirit in the next dimensions. Which was... borderline unfathomable.

It was one thing for me to take her there, through the mind. For me to guide her there, both of us departing together at the same moment in space-time. However, for her to spirit to leave her body and go... I had no idea where... It would literally be like finding a tiny needle in all the verses within this multiverse... And all those beyond...

Which. Are. *Infinite.*

Thankfully, once I found her... We could travel back together. And while that, too, was no small feat... At least we would be together, and I was highly experienced in traversing four dimensions. I had been birthed in the four dimensional worlds and lived there until... Until my own nexus mate destroyed one of the realms in which we lived.

Ahualei, who was once a compassionate goddess of the fourth sun, water, fertility, and motherhood. She was now the goddess of an underworld. A realm of her own making after my brother, Tezcaht, killed our children and her waters drowned the realms for her sun to then burn it to ashes.

When I'd left, all that was left of her was some vague remnant of her spirit form that lived in an unconscious state, sustaining her death realm where all those she had accidentally killed roamed. And hoping that one day, when our children passed on to the realms in the unfathomable beyond... That they would find their way back to her.

It was now, thanks to having taken on a three dimensional form, a *long* distant memory having occurred so many eons ago, before the fourth heat death of the sun- her sun- of our realm. We were currently living in the eleventh sun of this realm... And even I had no idea how to reconcile the two time-lines but... After she had annihilated our realm, with me in it, and chosen to become an underworld... my spirit- physically appearing to be nothing more than a photon of light- wandered realm to realm for an inconceivable amount of time, drifting in a seemingly aimless direction... until I finally reached a vast, dark singularity into which I was... for lack of a better word...

Shat out and re-birthed.

When I emerged on the otherside... I found myself in this universe. And had been breathed new life. And as my being began to grow and warm, and develop once again through space-time... I felt a distant pull. That led me to Terrenea, where I fell from the skies and plummeted to the earth.

And when I rose from the sea into which I'd crashed, I took on a form that the humans considered to be a god. To me, the term 'god' had always encompassed so much more than someone or something bound to a physical body with such limited senses... But to them... It was simply a relatively immortal being that had control over some modicum of power that could manipulate various elements or aspects of the universe, like me.

In my astral projection of space-time, when I finally reached the 'near-future' Aurelia, there were shockingly few potentialities that existed where she would actually return from a death in this realm where her beautiful female form would await her.

Two to be exact.

The first, was that we open up the doorway between realms. I didn't need to venture any furtuer into that option. I already knew the risks and there were entirely too many variables beyond that, that once that doorway opened, it was like the timeline fractured like the glass of a broken mirror. Trillions of innocents would surely die, which included all of us with them. It would simply be a matter of time in accordance with each variable.

Kyril and his uncle had no fucking clue what they were dealing with. Where as they only speculated, I knew what was on the side of that doorway between dimensions because, unbeknownst to me at the time, I had been one of the beings to actually travel through it. And if it opened again, entities from countless worlds would surely do the same. And while a great many of them were beings filled with awe-inspiring benevolence and love, many were not. They were beings of destruction, death, and suffering. Like Ahualei.

The second, required that I die and travel with Aurelia to the after realms so that I could navigate us back to this dimension, and to Aeternia because being in spirit form superseded any physical boundaries or necessity to open physical doorways or portals. Aurelia and I were, thankfully, bound by The Creators' Promise which- as I'd now discovered- was as powerful as the tether of a nexus mate. But in order for Aurelia and I to do this, I would have to risk us both surviving in Ahualei's underworld- although it was a world I would no longer recognize, it was where I had come from. She had been my nexus mate, after all. The other half of my soul. So of course, when I died... That was precisely where my spirit would go.

CHAPTER
FIFTEEN
AURELIA

T was free falling. In the dark. I couldn't have seen the back of my hand if I'd held it an inch in front of my face. And I was somehow supposed to keep my mind focused on a singular question.

As I was apparently plummeting to my death.

But the end never came.

I fell and fell, my stomach eventually evening out. Long seconds passed and as I caught my breath I grasped onto the words in my mind.

"How can I break Nuala's curse and we both continue to live?"

I repeated the question in my head so many times that the words became as jumbled as my brain as I spun and flailed in my descent.

Until finally, I was enveloped in a body of water. Still in pitch blackness, it took a few lung burning moments for me to realize which way was up or down. When I finally willed myself to calm, my body began to float upwards and I kicked my way back up to the surface.

I burst above the water, swimming in circles trying to strain my eyes in the darkness. Fear making my breaths come in quick pants as I prayed that their were no hungry predators in the vicinity.

Thankfully, the water was warm. Blue light rippled in my peripheral vision. I swished my arms through the water seeing that with each stroke, the surface of the water gave a faint illumination.

Déjà vu washed over me as I looked around in the darkness, swimming in what I hoped was the right direction as the blue light wasn't nearly enough to properly gauge my surroundings but... I'd been here before... In a dream. One that I'd only had a handful of days ago. Moments before Lussathir had kidnapped me by slipping a palladium collar around my neck and folding into Lux Dryadalis with me.

I tried to recall it but... All I could vaguely remember was this place, and eventually seeing various worlds in the distance, one that I could distinctly make out to be the one where Quetz had taken me to, to see my bother after he'd been killed. And that there'd been a winged male there... A naked one.

I continued to swim forward until my bare feet hit soft sand and I could walk. The water became increasingly shallow as I ventured on, until it was only an endless puddle beneath my feet.

"Aurelia...," a deep voice sounded behind me. I whirled to find a tall, powerfully built male striding leisurely toward me. An impressive set of golden wings were glowing behind him providing the only illumination in the room... or chasm. Wherever we were.

Unlike when I'd first met him, he was actually wearing trousers now. Though he remained shirtless. And if I wasn't currently barely managing to keep my panic leashed, I may have even been capable of admiring his handsome personage.

At this particular moment, however, I couldn't possibly give less of a shit.

"*You...*" The word came out both a question and a statement.

"I'm happy you found your way back to me."

"... I didn't choose to come here."

"No?"

"No... I entered The Waters of Kismet. And it took me here."

His brows drew together tensely but his expression remained unreadable.

"How is my son?"

A knowingness settled within me. Of course this was Kyril's father. It was no wonder why something about him seemed so familiar even if there faces were rather dissimilar.

My heart clenched painfully at the thought of my nexus.

"Unwell."

A frown saddled his face as he gave a knowing, forlorn nod.

"What question did you ask the waters?"

"I need to die so that I can save my best friend from an anima libera curse. But... I would like to go back after. To my life in Aeternia."

"To Kyril?"

My throat worked roughly as my own shame swallowed me whole.

Kyril's father offered me a compassionate smile. "My son has chosen his path... I do not blame you for wanting another."

Whether he meant 'another' path, or 'another' male, I wasn't sure but I couldn't bring myself to ask.

"I am sorry to say that... I do not know the answer. My domain lies in this realm. I may be the god of Aeternia's afterworlds but it lies even beyond my powers to bring them elsewhere. Even *if,* when you die, you were to come here, I wouldn't be able to simply 'fold' your spirit from this realm to a realm outside of here.

"I am bound here. I left once long ago, when those sigillums my son wants were first created. That is how I left. And I became trapped there, desperate to leave. Thankfully, after a few thousand years there, I met Kyril's mother. But with only a shadow of my powers, I was eventually killed. And my soul returned here to its former home.

I do not know how, nor wish, to go back. My nexus, Kyril's mother is here."

I shook my head in disbelief. How? *Why?* Why was I here if he didn't have the answer.

"If anything, I would imagine that being the guardian and guide of souls... That *you* of all beings would be able to come and go as you please between your worlds and the afterworlds."

I ground my molars together so hard my jaw began to ache.

If it only it were that simple.

It was merely an extension of my spirit that guided them beyond our worlds. I couldn't remember anything before I'd first taken form and been birthed, to parents I'd never known, on Terrenea.

And I had no idea how to navigate the realms beyond without my physical form to anchor me. If I severed that connection, and *killed* myself, I would become untethered from this realm and, to be honest, I had no idea where I would go.

Would I even come to Kyril's father's afterworlds?

Or would I go somewhere else?

My ancestors had also come through that doorway when the sigillums had first been created. But from where, I had no idea. Saying that just because I was basically 'the ferrywoman' of souls, guiding them to and from the afterworlds across a singular cosmic 'lake'... was like saying that I should be able to swim across the entire Atlantic Ocean on Terrenea, but if the Atlantic Ocean was *infinite*.

I shoved down my annoyance at his rather arrogant assumption.

"Much to my dismay, that too lies beyond my powers."

Kyril's father sighed heavily, his mouth tightening in a way that belied either his frustration at my finite capabilities, or frustration on my behalf. It made no difference to me which but I was definitely beginning to lose my patience, especially considering our rather imminent time constraints.

"You cannot use those sigillums to open that doorway between dimensions, Aurelia. If you do... The worlds, as you know them, will end."

"I know," I ground out, ready to snap.

My eyes wandered, desperate to find something, or perhaps *someone* else in this gods-forsaken cave or whatever it was. Someone else who may have an answer.

And soon.

For all I knew, Kyril was about to arrive and pull me out of here. Not that I had even the faintest idea of how that was possible.

"If you sever your nexus bond to him he will no longer strive to use the sigillums. And perhaps he will be alleviated of his madness."

My jaw dropped.

"What?"

"I said, 'If you sever-

"I heard what you said, it was a rhetorical 'what'. As in, 'What do you mean? How is that possible?'"

Kyril's father's jaw feathered and I felt a pang of guilt for snapping at him. He couldn't help that he was about as clueless as I was. However, he *had* just casually suggested I sever my tether to the other half of my fucking soul.

"The Shamaness, Morwen, should be able to do it."

Another phantom pain seared the tether between Kyril and I.

"And what becomes of us then?"

"I have only come across a handful of souls that have done such a thing. They... became shadows of their former selves. You would literally be losing the connection to the other half of your soul. For most, it drastically reduces their life span on Aeternia."

I huffed a mirthless laugh.

"And you would wish that upon us? Upon your son?"

"If it prevented Kyril from opening that doorway and saved the near countless lives of your realms... Yes."

Tears swelled in my eyes, out of hopelessness and fear that what he suggested may actually be necessary. Even after all Kyril had done... I'd still held some minuscule flicker of hope in my heart and in my subconscious...

That maybe in time, even if it were hundreds or even thousands of years in the future, that he could change. So much could change between now and then... We would surely be different people by then.

We were extremely young immortals. I hadn't even been consciously aware of the secret tiny hope I'd been harbouring until now. Until he suggested actually throwing it all away. Everything Kyril and I had been through together during the war... As my thoughts began to spin out of control, I realized we hadn't actually been together for long. Only a few short years before I'd been murdered in my sleep by Kyril's Uncle Caelus.

I shook my head, abandoning the downward spiral of my thoughts. There were more pressing matters to deal with and all I could hope was that wherever Quetz had hid those sigillums in the trench in that Terrrenean ocean would be enough. For now.

"I see you are bound to a creator's promise."

My gaze, previously lingering in the black distance, slammed back to his.

"... Yes."

"With whom may I ask?"

"... Quetzacoatl... God of the Winds, Rain, Time, The Arts, and All Good Things..."

Kyril's father's expression was pensive yet again unreadable and gave no sign as to whether or not he knew of him. His lips parted as if to respond but as soon as they did, the ground and water beneath my feet began to tremble. My panic shrieked anew.

"What are you doing?!"

Kyril's father's wings shot out to balance himself. His ire contorting his features and suddenly making him look almost identical to Kyril, with a snarl to match.

"This isn't me."

The sand beneath my feet dipped and sunk. I flung myself forward to escape as it began to pull me under. I cried out, clawing at the water and sand that only seemed to widen it's yawning maw further, determined to swallow me whole. Kyril's fathers wings heaved a great flap to prevent himself from being sucked in. He dove forward, grasping my arm in a bone-crushing grip but it was still not enough to pull me out. Terror widened his gaze to reveal the whites of his eyes as the quicksand began to pull him down with me, despite the powerful beats of his wings raging against it.

When it reached my neck, and his elbow, a look of guilt replaced his fear. His words came out barely more than a whisper.

"I'm sorry, Aurelia..."

And then he let go.

SIXTEEN

AURELIA

If I'd been able to open my mouth, or actually known his name, I would have cursed him. Instead, sand bearing the weight of a *sun,* and felt as though it were to trying to crush me like it had a vendetta, engulfed me.

Forced to hold my breath, my lungs felt set to burst.

Just as the shifting sands eventually *stilled.*

And if I thought I was panicking before, *this* was the kind of panic that would haunt you for the rest of your days. I'd been buried alive. The sand too tightly packed for me to draw my arms through. And with no air to breathe... There was no way I would survive before they sent Kyril to pull me out of the Waters of Kismet. Which had clearly been intent on killing me.

But as that thought filled my mind, I realised it didn't have to be in vain.

My life for Nuala's.

I repeated those words, praying that The Creator's, or someone or something would hear me. Tears spilled from the tightly shut slits of my eyes destined to water the sandy grave crushing me as I thought of Kyril and all his suffering, and I sent a silent prayer out for his tortured soul. *I'm sorry.* I'm sorry that this happened to you. That you'd suffered through so much you were willing to become a harbinger of suffering to others. I'm sorry that I wasn't able to save you.

And as my chest and lungs began to spasm and I could feel consciousness slipping from me, memories of all the time I'd been gifted with to share with Quetz washed over me and my heart filled to bursting with so much love, and now agony for all that I longed to share with him but now knew I never would. And I sent a silent prayer to him. *I love you.*

CHAPTER
SEVENTEEN
AURELIA

Cool water tickled the tips of my toes, drawing my attention. Or what was left of the consciousness of dying mind. The sensation of cool water rose steadily, engulfing my feet, my shins, and I could finally move. I began to kick with the last trickle, one that I didn't even know I'd had, in my reservoir of strength and all at once the sand around me gave way and I was tumbling in what felt like a crashing wave.

And was pummelled by it.

I opened my eyes to see... light. I was still underwater, getting *demolished* by these waves... but I could see. I kicked to swim to the surface, my head bursting above water, and *at last*, I finally took air into my lungs.

My breaths heaved in shrill gasps as I blinked the salty water from my eyes. When my breaths finally grew steady, I paddled in a circle looking for sign of land. But all I could see, barely managing to stay afloat in the choppy waves, was more water....

After a few moments, the choppy waves flattened as I felt a pulling sensation in the water behind me. I turned to find...

Oh fuck.

The water pulled harder, drawing me backward as it attempted to suck me into the massive tidal wave that was growing taller by the millisecond.

Instinct had me trying to escape by swimming away from it but I quickly realized my efforts were futile. I turned, taking in a deep lungful of breath, and dove *into* it. I swam as fast as I could deeper and deeper, in the hopes that I would be able to swim out of its watery grasp.

My efforts had come too late and my hopes were in vain. The tidal wave reached me and sucked me into another horizontal vortex of thundering, pounding waves. It propelled me forward at a speed that literally ripped my pants off before I was thrown onto the sharp, rocky boulders of the ocean floor. Bones snapped and blood spilled, but still it wasn't done with me.

My body continued to violently thrash forward against more rocks until they turned to sand... Or no... Until sand replaced the rocks, and air replaced the water. The waves pushed me forward further onto powder soft sand until I could crawl.

I picked my head up, coughing, spluttering, and vomiting water as I managed, on hands and knees, to make my way towards the sandy beach that the waves behind me gently nudged me toward

When I finally breached the shore, broken bones and all, I collapsed onto the sand. Now, more than grateful for consciousness to flee me.

EIGHTEEN

AURELIA

A soft hand caressed my cheek. Still half asleep, I nuzzled further into it.

A soft feminine chuckle had my eyes popping open, yanking me back to reality. My vision blurred and weaved, head spinning, before it finally settled on the face in front of me.

And an astoundingly beautiful face it was.

A female, surely not human, with long, thick, black hair that lay unfurled beyond her waist hovered beside me. Her lips were full, even fuller than mine, and a perfectly formed cupid's bow. High cheek bones and long black eyelashes framed large, doe eyes that sparkled like pale blue chips of ice. I couldn't stop my gaze as it wandered downwards, grazing over her pointed, petite chin, long, delicate neck, and slender shoulders... and beyond to her voluptuous, teardrop shaped breasts that were barely concealed by the low-cut white muslin dress that hugged her tiny waist.

She was, without a doubt, the most beautiful woman I had ever since. In this life and the one before it. And she had a voice to match.

It sounded the way silk feels against the skin. Light, smooth, soft, and airy.

She tilted her head, studying me curiously, sitting on the bed beside me.

"Hello..."

Too breathtaken by her beauty and the bizarre set of circumstances in which I'd arrived, I couldn't muster a response.

She tried again. "Who are you?"

I cleared my throat, suddenly feeling very self-conscious with all my gawking.

"Aurelia..."

Her brows furrowed. "Who?'

"I am known as the Goddess of Origin."

She quirked an eyebrow at me.

"I guide souls to the afterworlds."

A few moments passed as she seemed to consider this.

"How fascinating..."

She studied me further.

"And how do you know Quetzacoatl?"

My breath caught, stilling the wandering gaze that had been scanning the naturalistic but luxurious room around us.

The reaction seemed to greatly heighten her interest.

Her gaze became piercing as she waited, breath held, for me to answer.

"I... He's a dear friend of mine."

Her beautiful, gentle, and pillowy features suddenly sharpened.

"Is that so?" She asked quietly as her gaze ran over me, scrutinizing.

As if a mirror to her own, hideous jealousy suddenly reared within me.

How did he know this utterly beguiling and stunningly beautiful female?

Though part of me already knew the answer. And it hurt.

My words nearly came out accusatory. "Who are you?"

What I felt was a sickeningly smug smirk, but was probably just a very normal smirk, curled one corner of her obnoxiously beautiful mouth.

"My name is Ahualei. I am the Goddess of Water, Fertility, and... this realm's underworld," her features tightening at the latter words, "I am Quetzacoatl's nexus."

I studied her and all of her breathtaking perfection with nothing short of shameful disgust. Angry heat seared my veins not only at her, but the fact I couldn't find a single imperfection. I heaved a bitter sigh.

As if this journey couldn't have possibly been anymore painful or soul-crushing.

"Perhaps if he hasn't returned it's because he doesn't want to?" The words surely stabbing me more than they would her.

Or perhaps not. Her features darkened dramatically and suddenly she no longer looked so beautiful. Her voice no longer sounding light and airy but an otherworldly snarl.

"Bring him to me."

My jaw tightened. "I beg your pardon?"

Her words came out like oozing venom. "I smell him on you. I heard your mind call out to him. Bring him to me."

My brows drew tightly together. "And where are we exactly?"

"Miklan. The Underworld of the Ometäian realms."

A hell. *Great.* The words left my mouth before I could think any better of it.

"And what do you want with him?"

"He is my nexus. Who are you to ask what I wish to do with him?"

"I'm the one who's supposed to deliver him to you, no?"

The canines of her teeth lengthened and the veins her face surfaced in jagged streaks.

"I need him to come rule this realm with me."

"So you need his help?"

"If I am to ever leave this gods-forsaken realm, someone has to take my place. I have waited eons, more than even I can fathom, for my- *our-* children to join me."

My jaw dropped and a new kind of pain stabbed me. Quetz had children...

"You had children together?"

My heart throbbed painfully as if slamming it's head against my chest wall to knock itself unconscious.

Her lips twisted into a sadistic grin as she recognized my pain.

"We had two beautiful, perfect children... And his brother killed them."

Just when I thought it couldn't get any worse... Tears filled my eyes at imagining the pain he must have gone through.

"Where are they now?"

Her brows drew together into a grim line.

"I do not know."

I didn't dare tell her I could find them. Probably... I had never attempted to find beings of another dimension before. But when I returned, after we saved Nuala, I would definitely speak with him about it... Perhaps I could find them for him.

"And you wish to bring them here? To the underworld?"

"If they will not join me here, then I will join them wherever it is they are."

"So you want Quetz to take your place?"

Her eyes narrowed at my using a diminutive of his name before she suddenly burst into laughter.

"You love him don't you?"

I couldn't bring myself to deny it and it only made her laugh all the harder.

"Perhaps I'll let you live, and you can stay here with him, if you bring him to me."

I huffed mirthlessly.

"Well, unfortunately for me, I have no idea how to leave this place. And unfortunately for you, even if I could, I would have no idea as to how I could return with him even if I wished to do such a thing."

Creators, please, if you're listening, take me from this place.

Only Ahualei responded, a sinister smile curling her lips. "Well, *he* certainly does. If he actually loves you then surely he will come for you. Guards!"

My eyes swung to the bedroom, heart leaping at the sight of the towering ghastly shadows that moved *through* the door.

Before I could fold away from them, searing pain punctured my abdomen. A cry escaping me as I folded away from her, and back to the only place I knew here. The sand. I dropped to my knees at the shore, hands trembling as I slowly withdrew the blade from my abdomen. Blood spilled onto the sand- far more than such a slender blade should be able to draw. I willed my spirit to leave this place, to return to Aeternia.

But knelt in the sand, and in a dark pool of my own blood, I remained.

Ahualei folded only a dozen yards or so in front of me, along with her shadowy guards. I opened my mouth to let out a cry but instead only a wet gurgle escaped. Black liquid rose in my throat and spilled from my lips, even giving Ahualei and her guards pause.

I hunched over on my hands and knees, vomiting the black liquid, until it pooled around my hands and wrists. And the sand shifted, pulling me deeper into it.

Creators. Not again. Please.

The last thing I heard was Ahualei's shrill scream as the sand, yet again, swallowed me whole.

NINETEEN

QUETZACOATL

2 2 hours had passed so far.

And it had been the longest 22 hours of my entire life. I hadn't left this room but to relieve my body of its natural functions, hadn't eaten, hadn't slept, and I had begun to drink the wine Morwen had left for me since I'd insisted on staying in this room.

Kyril had come and gone, paced anxiously, seemed to be on the cusp of quite literally pulling his hair out, and stared daggers at me as though he'd hoped the effort would kill me.

During which, I had scoured the fragment of time in which Aurelia and I would soon have to journey. Not to mention that the journey would be an actual trip to hell. I also had no idea of what precise moment she would return. Only that she would, eventually, return. Without Kyril's help. I had explained this to Morwen and her only response had been, *"Would you like to be the one to tell him that he should leave his nexus because you've got everything under control?"*

I would have had no problem explaining this to him either but I knew it would only result in bloodshed. His mostly, and I had no desire to further upset Aurelia. I also suspected that, due to The

Creators' Promise that I'd sworn to Aurelia, and was bound by my very to soul to protect her, that I could also pull her out of the portal if need be but I didn't bother to vocalize this either. Again, lest it result in bloodshed that would only further distress her.

I had just flopped myself onto the nearest chaise longue, wine bottle in hand, when the black waters began to tremble, snapping my gaze to it's usually still surface and I could have sworn my heart stopped beating entirely. The wine bottle shattered as I released it and folded to stand beside the basin.

In the next breath, Aurelia burst through the surface choking on the inky substance. I reached in to haul her from its depths as she flailed desperately, and based on her appearance I didn't want to risk hurting her by grabbing her too firmly. Using my body as a shield from the floor's unforgiving surface, we both toppled to the ground. She gripped tightly onto the front of my shirt, her body contracting violently trying to expel the black liquid- and distinctly what appeared to be blood- from her lungs, onto my front.

I brought my arms around her to cradle her with increasing horror. My eyes roved her mostly naked body that was mottled heavily with bruises and gashes. What was left of her clothes were mere flaps of fabric. It looked as though they'd, literally, been torn from her body. My stomach churned at the sight and bile nearly rose in my throat as images of what circumstances would cause such a thing.

As she vomited the last of the blood and the black Waters of Kismet- which magically drew themselves back into the basin- she laid herself, face first, on top of my chest. I promptly folded with her into the guest room that Morwen had given me, her breaths coming in desperate pants, and magically sealed the room from being folded into.

We laid on the floor on an enormous fluffy rug, her body wilted over mine as her breaths finally evened out. I was desperate to find out what she'd experienced but it had clearly been something traumatizing and I was horrified to even ask.

Relief trickled into to my anxiety as I watched the wounds on her arms and legs gradually healing. But I could imagine that, not long ago, they'd been much worse. My relief was short-lived as her body began to spasm again with sobs that wracked her body.

I sat up, cradling her in my arms and pulling her body against my chest, as she still held a white knuckled grasp to the front of my shirt.

My heart shattered into a million pieces as she wept and it only took a few beats of my heart before my tears joined hers. My hands shook from the infinite horrors she could have experienced that my imagination was summoning.

When her sobs finally stilled her voice came out a raspy whisper. "How much longer do we have?"

Surprisingly, I managed a soft, gentle whisper that masked the pain in my voice. "About a day... How long were you there?"

"Perhaps two hours. Maybe less. Maybe more. I'm not entirely sure."

A swell of relief washed over me. At least she hadn't been trapped there for half an eternity. Though any number of nightmares could happen in the span of a couple hours... And based on her appearance, they apparently had.

She remained silent for several moments.

"Can I have something to drink?"

I promptly summoned a large goblet of water from Morwen's kitchen. She only released one hand from the front of my now bloody shirt to grab it as she gulped desperately at it, much of its contents spilling down the front of what was left of her shirt.

"More please," she gasped.

I summoned another goblet and when she finished it off she let it clang, empty, onto the wool rug before resuming the death grip she had on my shirt with both hands as she curled tighter against me.

"Please don't let go of me."

My heart shattered impossibly further.

"You'd literally have to kill me." Stomach churning with dread the moment the words left my mouth, knowing that she'd have to do precisely that in a matter of hours.

"We have time to sleep if you want."

I felt her head nod against me.

"I'd like to... shower first."

Folding directly into the now running shower, she finally released her grip on my shirt to grasp my shoulders as I set her down and knelt at her feet to pull off the tattered remains of her clothes. When I finished, I wrapped my arms tightly around her legs and held on, clutching her against me. She wove her fingers through the wet locks of my hair and I could have wept in relief at the action alone.

Gradually, I began to wash her... Scrubbing and washing every part of her perfect body- perfect, not from a lack of imperfections but because those imperfections made her all the more perfect- with more tenderness than I'd ever mustered for anyone in this lifetime. Never once letting go of her entirely, always anchored to her with one hand or the other, and pressed firmly against my body, just as much for her reassurance as it was for mine. And finally, when I finished rinsing her and dried both of us off and carried her to bed.

With her body pressed firmly against mine, it wasn't until I felt her breathing become slow and steady, that I could finally drift off to sleep with her.

TWENTY

QUETZACOATL

Despite the macabre and gruesome nightmares that had peppered my dreams, wholly inspired by the day that lay ahead, I had still managed to sleep deeply. Aurelia still laid cocooned in my arms and curled against my chest, her legs woven with mine.

The sun had nearly risen, and dread had begun to bloom in my chest as my thoughts wandered to the time when it would set and we would have to leave this heavenly sliver of space-time where we were alone and sequestered away from the horror that awaited us. *But we would soon return,* I chided myself.

According to the visions I'd seen in my scrying, I knew that when we made this journey together, once on the other side, time would seem to pass as usual- however long it took- but *when-* I reminded myself, not *if-* we returned to our bodies, that to everyone else, it would seem like hardly anytime at all had passed. Which is precisely what I kept telling myself. *Technically, it'll only be a few minutes.*

· · ·

Full lips pressed against my chest, making my heart swell, and snapping my thoughts back to the present. I looked down to find Aurelia kissing the smooth, broad plains of my chest. Her lips pulled back as her mouth reached my nipple and she gave it a gentle nip. Uncertainty, and arousal, stirred within me. My words came out a groan as my cock thickened and grew with each lash of her tongue and press of her lips.

"Aurelia... Are you... Feeling well?"

Her lips stilled to meet my gaze, eyes glistening.

"I don't want to leave this world never having had the gift of loving you."

Even as her words made my heart fill to bursting, I felt my cock's hardening instantly wane. In only a few hours, she would have to die. However briefly. And the only thing that was holding me together, though it was only by a thread, was the fact that I was going with her. Even if we failed to return, at least we would be together. Even if it was adrift in a distant realm, in a distant corner of space-time...

We could find another realm to dwell in. Together... And the sound of that didn't sound so bad at all. As long as she would be ok with it. Nothing sounded bad to me so long as we were together.

I searched her gaze feeling desperate. Creator's knew that I wanted to *love* her. In so many more ways than one for the rest of eternity if she'd have me.

"*Stop,*" she pleaded, "I know you're thinking of everything that lies ahead of us today. Of all the horrors you're imagining I just went through. And yes, it was horrible and I never want to see a fucking grain of *sand* ever again..."

My brows furrowed at her words, each one more panicked and desperate than the last.

"*But I don't care.* I want to spend every fucking second cherishing this time we have together. And I don't want to a waste a single moment of it worrying about the future. We have *now...*"

She sat up abruptly, hands planted firmly on my chest as her tears began to fall and her beautiful face reddened with her fervor.

"Because that's all we ever have. And right now, we *have* each other. And *that* is a fucking *gift* that I will not waste. I may not be able to control virtually *anything* in this world, clearly, but I can decide how I choose to spend my time. And I'll be damned if I squander this precious gift doing anything other than showing you how much I love you. How grateful I am for you."

Tears swelled in my eyes as I listened to her words, turning into borderline frantic pants as though her words were fighting for dominance against her breath.

"For spending 33 years trapped in a fucking mirror, in a gods-damned dungeon. For being there for me in my darkest hour when nothing and no-one else in this world could have consoled me but you. By reuniting me with my brother's spirit. For vowing to-

I sat up, crashing my mouth into hers with more force than I'd intended. Still, she threw her arms around my neck as I wrapped her in mine and laid her beneath me. Her legs parted before twining them around my waist, gifting the underside of my now throbbing length with the press of the soft, wet heat of her core. Purely out of mindless need, I thrust forward sliding my cock through her wet folds. And *gods* she was wet. The idea alone had me ready to explode.

And the cry of ecstasy she made in response, nearly undid me. She reached between us to grab my length and align it with her core but I stilled, making her efforts futile.

TWENTY-ONE

AURELIA

" **I** recall you saying something about cherishing," Quetz said smoothly, his voice sounding like liquid gold as he pressed open-mouthed kisses to my breasts, nipping, licking, and *teasing* one as his long fingers caressed the other.

What was he saying?

The river of my thoughts had completely run dry, and the rest of me had become nothing more than a sopping, wet puddle of writhing and moaning need.

As he finally brushed his thumb over my nipple, his mouth closed over the other, groaning as he did so, and flicked his tongue over its tightened peak. He began to *slowly* slide his *enormous*, and jaw droopingly beautiful, hard length back and forth through my wet folds. Creating the most perfect, wet friction against my clit that had a powerful tingling heat rising within me and my core clenching greedily.

My breaths were already coming in uneven, staccato pants peppered with soft high-pitched moans. I could feel my climax already rapidly approaching. My hips began to thrust in counter to his earning me a chuckle.

At once he stilled and the proof of my frustration and need dug itself into the flesh of his back with my nails. *"Please,"* I begged, as his kisses drifted from my breasts down the soft expanse of my stomach. He hummed his pleasure thoughtfully, his deep voice resonating within me and making my toes curl and point with pleasure.

"If I let you cum now, will you promise to let me make you cum again after?"

The words alone made me moan, hips writhing as I sank my fingers into the soft, luscious curls of his black silken hair. Quetz reached my core and groaned his pleasure, tenderly grazing his nose against my outermost folds and inhaling deeply. I cried my response, core clenching. *"Yes."*

Quetz slid his hands around the tops of my thighs and pulled me against his mouth. His tongue firmly licked up my slit, and everywhere around it, as though he were trying to devour every last drop of my wetted essence. The proof of my need for him. Once satisfied he'd sufficiently laved me, he pressed a finger to my slit and gently slid the digit inside me pulling another sweet moan from me. He curled his other hand around my thigh to reach between my legs and part my folds before returning to his oral ministrations.

What began as featherlight, steady flicks of his tongue gradually increased to firm, passionate lashings. A steady and unending stream of both curses and affectionate positive affirmations spilled from my lips as I desperately tried to hold back my orgasm. After all, it had only been perhaps *a minute and a half.*

A cry tore from my throat as Quetz added a second finger and his lips closed around my clit and *sucked,* somehow still managing to steadily whip his tongue against it simultaneously. And *oh my gods...*

I *detonated.*

· · ·

It felt as though my body, mind, and soul burned like the stars and exploded into a supernova. Quetz's ministrations gradually slowed, in utterly synchronistic timing as he gently guided me down from the heavens of my climax and returned me to Morwen's guest bedroom. I opened my eyes, all of two minutes after we'd begun and stared at him in utter awe.

"What the fuck was that?" The words poured out of me, just as bewildered as I was. Quetz's brows drew together with concern, lips parting in shock and still glistening with my wetness, briefly before bursting into laughter. He crawled his way back up to me, kissing, licking, sucking, and biting his way up every dip and curve of my body. Chuckling his mirth until his laughter turned to groans and my silence turned to moans.

"You have a promise to keep, Aurelia..."

When his mouth reached mine, I slid my body out from beneath his and guided him to sit on the edge of the bed. When I knelt before him, nestled between his legs, the erect, glorious length of him stood eye level with me.

Sweet, merciful gods.

Quetz's lips parted and his breathing stilled as I stared up at him, into the turquiose depths of his oceanic eyes. Being the center of his attention drew a feline grin to my lips that I didn't care to suppress.

"Breathe, Quetzacoatl."

A corner of his perfect mouth quirked up in response even as something like awe filled his gaze.

I wrapped my fingers around the towering length of him, and I couldn't even close them. I still had a good couple centimeters or so left to bridge the gap. I sucked on my cheeks, trying to draw as much saliva as I could muster to the front of my mouth before pulling Quetz's length down towards my mouth so that I could add it to the glistening beads already pearling at the tip of it.

My eyes locked with his as I *spat* the ball of saliva, and I felt no small amount of satisfaction watching the way the pupils of his eyes flared wide with need, and his fists white-knuckled in the bedsheets.

My grin curled wider as I brought my hand to the crown of him to spread it over its glistening surface.

Abs tensing, his breaths became shallow pants of anticipation. And with the first pump of my hand that stroked down the thick, godly pillar of him, a deep moan escaped his throat. But it still wasn't wet enough. So I reached between my thighs, seeking the wetness he'd so masterfully coaxed from my body, drawing my fingers through my folds to add it to our... potion. I couldn't help but giggle at the thought as I worked it over him.

Our eyes met and his already parted lips smiled softly. My heart gave a tender flutter of the wings Quetz had given it.

"Gods, Aurelia... I love you."

His eyes glittered with emotion and his words had come out a deep, breathy groan. And although his admission, however obvious it had long been in his actions, made my own emotion swell inside me. And I was determined to make the most of our time together.

Stroking him at a leisurely, exploring pace I began to press my passion against his hardened flesh in open-mouthed kisses, before licking up his length, holding his gaze all the while. His body had begun to tremble beneath me.

When I reached his crown, I hesitated, unabashedly licking my lips staring into his heavy-lidded eyes. My voice took on a velvety timber I barely recognized.

"If I let you cum now, will you promise to let me make you cum again after?"

He let out a husky chuckle, caressing my cheek with his thumb as he seemed to explore me with new eyes.

I pressed my lips to the underside of his broad crown, licking and sucking the head of him into my mouth as I finally began to work him in earnest, but stroking still in that lazy way. Before I dove throat first onto him.

"*Fuuuuuuuck,*" Quetz groaned loudly, sliding a hand through my hair to fist my waves and keep them from obstructing the path the I was stroking, and sucking, up and down his length- that required *both* of my hands.

And *gods,* he was delicious.

Much like his scent, he tasted of summer rain but with a hint of citrus and a dark, musky sweet like a rich agave. Each time I reached the peak of him, my tongue laved the tip of him as my closed fists slid up to meet it before bobbing backdown to the base of him- or as far as I could reach- pushing him hard against the back of my throat.

I felt him hardening impossibly further in my mouth and hands, and if that wasn't enough of an indication, the trembling of his thighs and tensing his stomach made it undeniable that he was very quickly ascending to his climax.

But before I could greedily drain him of the wet essence I had now grown desperate to taste and swallow, he pulled me off of him. I landed on the bed beneath him, our mouthes crashing in a bruising kiss as he caged me in his arms- one anchored beside my head as the other roved over my curves. His long, talented fingers caressed their ascension of my breast before sweeping over their hardened peaks, making my core clench with need.

My hands wandered the unyielding expanses of his muscles, nails grazing. And although the words weren't sexy, they left my mouth before I could stop them.

"I'm so grateful for you, Quetzacoatl..."

Quetz hummed deeply, burying his face in the curve of my neck before blessing my lips and tongue with another kiss that coaxed another moan from my soul.

"Auriela, I'd have waited an eternity for you in that dungeon if it meant that I'd have you waiting for me at the end of it."

Sweet emotion filled my chest to bursting, the evidence of it burning my eyes as Quetz sat back on his heels. His gaze, now mirroring the glistening in my own, roved over every inch of me as though he were trying to commit it to memory.

He wove the long fingers of his hand with mine as he fisted his length in his other before painting it across my wet folds. Our eyes met and breath caught with all the love that I knew we shared.

Slowly, he pressed the broad crown of his magnanimous length against my core and I couldn't help but clench in anticipation. A grin curled a corner of his parted lips, his voice a deep husk.

"I'll never fit if you do that."

I willed myself to take a deep breath, the tension in my body easing on the exhale. He took the opportunity to push himself slightly further in, gently easing the head of him back and forth, gradually stretching me. When the whole of his crown was inside me, a whimper left me as my core spasmed with pleasure and the sweetest pain. Both dragging a groan from deep within him. A tremor had begun in his hands as he squeezed the generous flesh of my hips with barely held restraint.

His words came out a growl. "*You're going to break me.*"

I grasped his forearms firmly and thrusted my hips forward to take in a few more inches of him, and something like a cry and moan tore from my throat.

"*Only if you promise to do the same to me.*"

And with that, Quetz thrust the rest of the way inside me causing my back to arch off the bed as a tingling wave of pleasure crashed over me, and something like a breathy scream clawed its way out of me. Quetz's thrusts became long and steady, each one pulling more moans and whispers of promises, curses, and encouragement that proved to increase and *harden* his pace. Gazes held and searching as we explored this newly discovered territory between us.

Within only a few moments I felt my climax already approaching, my core clenching firmly around him. The action caused him to slow, and he thread an arm beneath my waist, pulling me up off the bed and against his chest. I let my legs straddle him, heels anchoring me to the bed as I countered each of his thrusts with one of my own.

He brought his free hand to my neck, both collaring my throat and firmly framing my jaw with his thumb and forefinger as he drew my mouth against his.

"Tell me you're mine, Aurelia. Even if it's just for now. In this moment. I need to hear it."

The words returned that sweet sting to my eyes.

"I'm yours, Quetz. In this moment and every moment we're gifted with in the future."

I drew back to make certain that he believed my words to be true and I saw all my emotion mirrored in his eyes. My body tightened, core clenching again, as I slammed myself harder against him. As my voice sung my body's, my heart's, and my soul's euphoria. Quetz drew his tongue across his thumb before reaching between us and and caressing his love for me in pussy-spasming circles against my clit.

Something blossomed and unfurled deep within me, within my soul and the infinite beyond, and poured out of me in heart-rending waves through the tether between us that made every hair on my body rise with electricity.

Quetz's hard thrusts turned merciless and I felt his essence begin to spill inside me. It filled me in waves that I swore reached so deep within in me, his seed took root in my soul. Tears spilled from my cheeks and, in response, he wrapped me in his arms as our thrusts slowed, kissing and licking the tears from my cheeks.

As we slowly drifted back down to our bodies, Quetz laid me beneath him, still seated deeply inside me. He buried his head between my breasts and caged my body in his strong arms. My fingers dove into the short unruly mane of his hair as my other hand reached for one of his, drawing it to my lips and pressing a firm, lingering kiss to the centre of his palm in another attempt express all the love and gratitude I had for him that I knew words alone would never be able to express.

Quetz pulled my hand to his mouth to reciprocate the action but instead of returning my hand to me, he threaded his fingers through mine and held it firmly against his cheek. And gradually our breathing slowed and our eyes slipped shut.

TWENTY-TWO

AURELIA

A firm, short knock wrenched me from my sacred slumber. *Kyril,* my magic confirmed for me. That knock was... far less aggressive than I'd have imagined considering the fact that he most likely knew who I was with in here but my heart began a furious beat in my chest none-the-less. Quetz rose, his clothes appearing on his previously naked body.

"Quetz," I shook my head, "Let me get it."

He stopped, giving me a cautious look. "You're sure?"

I folded in front of him and pressed my lips against his to soothe the tension tightening his brow. "Yes."

Despite my nauseous anxiety and foreboding tension, I quickly slipped a linen tunic and trousers on before opening the door.

Kyril stood in front of me with darkening circles under his eyes, his expression tight but it didn't at all have the fury I'd anticipated. Instead, it looked defeated. And despite everything he'd done... I felt like my heart was being torn out and the burning sensation of the tether between us that had oscillated between un-ignorable and utterly crippling, reared to life.

And based on the look on his face- he was feeling it too.

"Kyril..."

"I saw that Quetz had left Morwen's study... I just wanted to come check on you. Make sure you were still... You."

I nodded, swallowing roughly as I tried to find words.

I couldn't.

Kyril's eyes roved over me, and I knew that whatever he may have suspected was confirmed. The look on his face hardened to steel and for the first time, his eyes, that had so recently held so much heat and passion, and... whatever his version of love was... became cold.

"Well. I see that you're alive... Did you get your answers?"

My breath caught at the question. Having just been ripped from sleep in these brief moments before I'd opened the door, I'd been too busy trying to kept my head above the waves of dread at having to *die* in a matter of hours. At simply facing Kyril after what had happened between Quetz and I, and the fiery burning of our presumably dying tether.

With all of that taking the forefront, I'd effectively managed to bury my trip through The Waters of Kismet, for the moment, behind me.

Everything regarding his father came rushing back to me and the words spilled from me before I could think better of it.

"I met your father."

His tan face paled dramatically, along with its hardened expression which evaporated instantly.

I'd asked Kyril, Morwen, and Nox to join me and Quetz in *Batlaan's* study. I couldn't muster the strength to even think about going anywhere near The Waters of Kismet ever again, much less stand in the same room with it less than 24 hours later.

· · ·

I paced the room, practically wearing a hole into the dark wooden floor boards, as I explained everything that had happened during my journey through The Waters of Kismet.

Although, I'd decidedly left out the part about Kyril's father advising me to have Morwen sever mine and Kyril's nexus bond. I didn't have the emotional capacity to deal with the fallout that would ensue- for both of us- to even consider or mention it, at the moment.

Kyril had stood nearby, shifting as I did, desperate to catch every unspoken detail on my face that I spoke about his father. Now that I knew they were related, I could see they held a moderate resemblance in their tan skin, dark hair, a similarly sharp jawline, tall and powerful build but having seen the two of them up close, I realized Kyril must have taken a lot of his mother's looks. Not to mention, Kyril didn't have a massive pair of glowing golden wings.

Still, I found their resemblance mildly unsettling. There was something about Kyril's *air*, his expressions, his magic that rung the most similar. And it made me feel like I was about to be swallowed whole again by that fucking sand. It would be a *long* time before I would be able to tolerate the feel of sand. If ever. Which was heartbreaking considering how much I loved the ocean and the seas. The beach.

Nox was the first to speak when I finished, sat in a cushy lounge chair with Morwen sitting on his lap looking very much like the king of the castle. Even though he wasn't. At least not at this particular castle.

I'd never seen him in his princely crown but I could easily imagine it with his sharp, elegant features, confident air, and the powerful magic he radiated.

"Well, using the sigillums was never an option anyway, so *that* wasn't terribly helpful. You're sure he didn't say anything else?"

Kyril seemed to hold his breath as he waited for me to answer.

"No..."

Kyril's eyes narrowed, surely detecting my lie, but he didn't push the matter. Not yet anyway.

Nox shook his head, roughly rubbing at his jaw that hadn't seen a razor in a few days but still looking no less regal.

"And why in all the hells would it take you to... Quetz's crazed nexus' underworld? What does that have to do with you?"

Kyril's jaw seemed to clench so hard I was surprised he didn't crack a tooth. And I didn't have an answer.

But it was Quetz who finally spoke.

"Because I have to die with her in order for her to make it back."

My jaw nearly hit the floor so hard it should have broken through the floorboards.

Both Kyril and I asking the same shocked, *"What?"*

"Why *you?* If anyone should go with her, it should be her nexus." Kyril growled.

Quetz heaved a sigh as though speaking to a child who had asked a question with an obvious answer. "Because if you go with her, you'll both be left to find your way back from whatever realm's after-world your ancestor's are from- which are two very different places, I imagine you realize-

I didn't realize at all actually considering I had no idea who my parents from my first incarnation were but we didn't have time to discuss it so I made a mental note to ask him about it later.

"- So, depending on the state of your *bond,* it's a gamble as to where you'll both end up. And let's say best case scenario, you do end up in the same afterworld, and you somehow find a way to leave-which is no small feat and nigh-impossible- your souls would be pulled adrift throughout the infinite sea of the cosmos for an unfathomable and indeterminable amount of time. And your greatest prayer would be that by some cosmic coincidence, you just happened to stumble upon a singlularity in the fabric of space-time through which you could travel through. And then, *if* you survived, you may or may not end up being *shat out and rebirthed* in the same dimension. And again! Let's say, *best case scenario,* by some fucking miracle of The Creators, *you actually did-*

Quetz's voice had steadily rose in intensity throughout his mind-boggling and *infinitely* terrifying explanation, and had now risen to a volume and fervor that could be considered borderline hysteria. What made it even more unnerving was the fact that I had never even seen him raise his voice before. He was always so playful, and relaxed, and sure, sometimes animated and expressive but never shouting and hysterical.

" - end up in the same dimension, in the same exact realm- which, again, would be an *absolute fucking miracle-* you'd have to find a way to leave again- and so on and so forth, until after potentially trillions of years- again, *if* you survive- you may or may not find your way back to this dimension. To this realm. To your bodies. And do you know what you would turn into then? If you did make it all this way but couldn't find your bodies because your consciousness became so far disconnected- thanks to the potentially trillions of years and what with all the shitting and rebirthing through the cosmic singularities, and all the other realms and dimensions you'll have to pass through- from anything that resembled your current self and would probably no longer even recognize its former 'immortal shell'. That is to say if this entire fucking realm hasn't burned down by then, *of course,*" he added pointedly, "because I can guarantee you don't but you'll be fucking *delighted* by the answer."

At our silence, he finally answered.

"A mute."

TWENTY-THREE

AURELIA

I f I hadn't been too busy having an internal meltdown, I'd have actually been proud of myself for not *shitting my pants* because if I hadn't been terrified before, I certainly was now.

And even if I hadn't found everything Quetz had just explained immeasurably daunting, becoming a mute was inconceivable. The term 'mute' referred to a being who had come to this world from another dimension- which dimension specifically, I had no idea- in an incorporeal form and had to *steal* a corporeal form. Meaning they had to kill someone, unless they just happened to be nearby when someone died, in order to gain a corporeal form. Otherwise, they'd be forced to wander the realms without access to the five physical senses. Even emotion was something that escaped them without their corporeal form. They existed purely on instinct and the need for... *life.*

And I actually felt some kind bizarre relief that Kyril actually looked nearly as afraid as I did. Perhaps now he'd reconsider trying to open that doorway between realms.

Kyril's next words, however, incinerated my tiny sprig of relief. In true form, obviously.

"Doesn't that stand for even more reason why we should open the doorway between realms?"

Quetz tossed his head back with a burst of maniacal laughter. "Ya know- I am *so* glad you brought that up, actually, because if you think you're gonna be able to open that gateway, you're fucking delusional. And even if you did succeed, you surely wouldn't live long enough to tell the tale because there are beings out there with power beyond your wildest dreams. And some- *some*- are benevolent. But there are others that would happily burn this world down, with you in it.

"And do you know what? They could do it in an instant. It wouldn't happen over the course of some long, drawn out war where you fight with your tiny, little swords, and you use your sparkly little powers- like your fire, and your ice, and your lightning- because there are some beings that *live* in that. It's all they know. It's their home. It's their life's blood. And they could destroy us all in the blink of an eye."

Nox sat slack-jawed. Even Morwen seemed to be in awe listening to Quetz's impassioned speech. And *finally*, a trickle of doubt flickered in Kyril's painfully dimmed gaze. And it still awed me that same gaze, less than a week ago, had been so bright and fiery and alive, and in love.

Kyril shook his head with something that looked like despair and disdain had gone hand-in-hand and leapt into a lake of ice.

"And how would you know exactly?"

Worry for Quetz bloomed in my chest as he tossed his head back with another maniacal laugh that made the last maniacal laugh look simply dead pan. This was *true* hysteria.

Kyril, Nox, Morwen and I watched on in shock and awe as Quetz continued to laugh until tears began to spill from his eyes.

"How would I know?" More hysterical laughter.

Morwen and I exchanged a nervous look.

"How would *I* know?"

Quetz was now doubling-over with his crying laughter, his voice becoming high-pitched.

"How would I know...." Quetz shook his head in disbelief, as he covered his face with his hands, and his crying laughter waned into just crying. Tears swelled in my eyes watching him.

I swiftly closed the distance between us and laid my hands on his shoulders, rubbing soothing circles on his back, as I spoke to him in the softest, gentlest tone I'd ever used with anyone.

"Hey... It's ok... You made it. Whatever happened, back then... it's in the past."

Finally, his watery gaze lifted to mine, tears pouring. And I felt a pang of pride that he was so unabashed and fearless in letting everyone see. His lips trembled and he bit his cheek as he held his head high and stared into my eyes.

And my own eyes began to swell not only with all the worry and fear at what had perhaps happened in that distant past. But with all the love, gratitude, and awe I felt for how truly wonderful and extraordinary he was.

"You're here *now*... Remember?"

A small smile trembled in one corner of Quetz's beautiful mouth before he slowly drew in a shuddering breath, nodding.

I threw a barrier around us as I removed what space remained between us and slid my arms over his shoulders and around his neck, pulling him gently against my chest. He wove his arms around me, burying his head in the curve of my neck. I felt his diaphragm begin to spasm as he sobbed quietly against me.

Tears spilled down my cheeks as I held him in my arms and continued to rub soothing circles on his back.

"*Shhhhhh.* You're here now. *We're* here now. Ok?"

Slowly, he finally lifted his head, eyes red and puffy, and pulled a hanky out of thin air. Blowing his nose before he willed it away again.

"Sorry," he whispered.

I reached up to hold his head in my hands and stared straight into his eyes trying to cement the truth of my words so that it might help him heal.

"Don't you ever be sorry for that. I love you. You've been through more than I could even begin to fathom. And I know it's hard, and it hurts, and sometimes you just wanna give up. And it's ok to feel that way. So long as you don't give up. Because we need you. *I* need you. And whatever happened, however you ended up here- through the unfathomable and orchestrated chaos of the universe- it's ok now because you survived and it lead you exactly where you're supposed to be. Right here to this moment. Which is '*an absolute fucking miracle'.*"

Quetz and I both burst into a teary laugh before both of our faces contorted grotesquely again- yes, even Quetz's face of godly perfection- as we both released a sound that was both a choked sob and a laugh. I pulled him hard against me and *squeezed*, desperately pushing all the love in the world down the tether of our Creator's Promise into him. I buried my face into the crook of his neck, just as his had returned to mine and whispered another truth.

"You're such a gift, Quetz."

TWENTY-FOUR

AURELIA

T he sun was now setting and the new moon, though it remained unseen to the naked eye was approaching its zenith at a pace that was both heartbreakingly fast, and gut-wrenchingly slow.

I had never been more terrified in my entire life. Even more terrified than I had been that night, that felt like it had occurred worlds ago, when I'd finally escaped Pauperes Domos and watched everyone I knew and love die, including my brother, because I'd blindly lead them to The Sable Forest to unwittingly meet their doom.

The same night that Quetz had spent 33 years in a dungeon waiting for me to arrive so he could take me to my brother's spirit in the afterworld to console me, and so that it would plant the seed necessary for us to become bound in a Creator's Promise.

And why all of that was so necessary exactly... I wasn't quite yet sure. And though I'd never have wished that fate upon anyone- to be trapped in an enchanted mirror, in a dungeon, for 33 years- I was eternally grateful to have him.

. . .

Here. By my side. Even though I knew that what I had to do next would hurt him. And perhaps in this way, Kyril and I weren't so different. It seems I'd been made a liar. Because I knew that what I was about to do would completely and utterly shatter him. But I was going to do it to protect him.

Morwen, Nox, and Kyril stood beside us as Quetz and I stood hovering beside Nuala's bed. Hesitating to the last moment to meet our potential doom. Kyril was beside me. His jaw feathered with determination to hold back tears. His words were one last desperate attempt. "She wouldn't want this for you... To risk it."

I knew that his words came from a place of fear. As all selfish, wounding actions do. Because he had reached a point where he had suffered so much that he simply couldn't anymore. Not if he could avoid it.

But as Aelia had recently said, *'The things we do to avoid suffering, often become the very cause of it.'*

I didn't have the words or the time to argue so I just offered him the only thing I could. A sad smile as I slipped my hand over his fore-arm, making the dying tether between us burn and flicker like a dying ember in the breeze. I reached my tip toes to whisper words that only he could hear as I pressed a kiss to his cheek.

"I'm sorry for all the pain its caused you but know that I am grateful for that precious thing we once had. No matter what's happened, I do love you. And I hope that one day soon you can find your courage again..."

I laid down beside Nuala on her bed. The anima libera had truly taken its toll. Her beautiful fiery red hair had paled to white and her skin had withered like a century old human's. The sight alone had made me choke back a sob. Though it served to strengthen my resolve for what I was about to do. Propped up on my elbow and staring down at her, I spoke to her mind-to-mind, hoping that she was somewhere listening.

"*I might not be here when you get back but... Please remember that I love you. So, so, so much. Please take care of Quetz.*"

I gave a silent nod to Morwen and Nox that tried to express more than I had the words or time to express but I hoped they understood none-the-less. Morwen's eyes glistened, her words seemingly spoken just as much for her own well being as it was for mine.

"You'll be right back. Don't worry."

I willed a trembling smile to my face, trying, and failing, to muster the confidence I didn't have.

I laid back beside her as Quetz joined, laying down next to me, and I grabbed one of his trembling hands and held it in mine as I turned on my side to face him.

I willed The Blade of Charon into my hands- the blade that Kyril had gifted me only a few short weeks ago.

The same one that his mother had given him before she died and had come into her possession because she'd taken in a seemingly fatally wounded male she'd found in the woods.

The one who'd bled liquid gold and had given it to her to say 'thank you' before he disappeared as quickly as he had come.

The blade that could kill any immortal with a single prick by severing the tether between the soul and its body.

Quetz laid on his side and brought my hand to his mouth. I tried to memorize the feeling of his lips pressed against my skin. The feeling of his love encompassing me. His strong hands to steady me. His magic twining with mine.

His eyes searched mine, his voice shaky with nerves.

"You ready?"

I took a deep breath. *Holy fuck, I most definitely was not.*

But I nodded anyway.

He took a shuddering breath, squeezing my hand one last time as he spoke.

"I love you. I'll be right behind you. And no matter what happens, we'll have each other."

I bit my cheek so hard it bled as I nodded again.

"I love you, Quetzacoatl. More than all the stars, in all the verses."

Time and space seemed to narrow down to one singular point as I brought that blade to my finger and gave it a single prick before willing it safely away and out of his reach.

Quetz's ensuing desperate, panicked cry faded in the distance rather quickly as a single bead of blood blossomed on the tip of my finger. Although I felt his hands grab me and shake me, my body grew numb as his arms came around me. He pulled me against his chest, his tears falling from his face onto mine as he wept, cradling me in his arms.

"Please, you have to let me come with you. It's the only way for you to come back."

I cupped his cheek with my hand with what last threads of control I still had in my body.

"Have some faith in the orchestrated chaos..."

TWENTY-FIVE

KYRIL

S omething within me died. From the moment Aurelia had pricked her finger with the blade I had given her. The one my own mother had given me to gift to her, my nexus mate, long before I'd ever even met her. And although I felt heartbroken, and the tears in my eyes fell in a ceaseless deluge for Aurelia, what we had, what she had chosen to do, everything that I had been through because of her and for her. And yes, admittedly, for myself.

Despite having been renowned as the infamous 'Burning Warrior' and the most powerful warrior in Aeternia, due to my efforts and successes in the war... I had lived my entire life in fear. It was all I knew.

I'd been raised in The Sable Forest, where only the most ferocious and inherently wicked of creatures dared to live, and *could* live in relative peace. Even if it was only peace *after* the violence their existence brought to others outside the forest.

My mother and I had fled there alone after my father, who I only just found out was the God of the Aeternian Afterworlds, had been murdered when I was a baby.

I'd met Nuala in that forest.

She'd been wandering it, stuck for months in her Chimera form after she'd killed Emperor Orova and escaped his harem.

She'd tried to kill me, and I'd driven my sword into her heart. Which had unexpectedly forced her back into her fae form. She'd looked so beautiful and vulnerable. And... *naked.* I hadn't had the heart yet to bring my sword down on her neck and burn out her heart.

When she'd healed and... apologized for having tried to *eat* me... I took her in. We'd become best friends. Her predilections had lay mostly with women at the time, though it always oscillated with her, and she was possibly the most sexually indiscriminate person I'd ever known.

I'd been so fucked up and... coincidentally, only interested in fucking... That nothing had ever happened between us. And then after many years of living in the comfort and peace of one another's company as she recovered from the trauma and horror of living the first 300 years of her life in that harem, and we readied for war, she introduced me to Morwen. Who then introduced me to Aurelia. Only a handful of years before my Uncle Caelus had killed her.

Whatever it was that had just died within me, didn't cause any tremendous pain. It was like a flame that had simply been blown out.

I looked down at The Blade of Charon that I now held in my hands, in my bedroom, at my home in The Northern Guard- or what remained of it- since the last time I'd been here, with Aurelia... Only a couple of weeks ago.

My mind spun with all the possibilities this blade could bring as I considered using it on myself. The moment after she'd pricked her finger it had appeared in my hand. No one had even noticed because they'd been so focused on their best friend and greatest ally dying before their very eyes. The words she'd spoken to me in my mind at that moment had hit me like the sledgehammer of destiny.

"For Caelus."

For Caelus. My uncle who had been the cause of the last 200 years of my suffering. The man that had murdered her to manipulate me into joining him in collecting the sigillums. The sigillums that he wanted so that he could return home. He'd been one of the few beings that had survived thousands of years after having come through that doorway between dimensions when 'the originals' had first opened it and arrived. And conquered.

Quetz had bellowed his torment, clutching Aurelia to his chest as though she were *his* nexus mate. The sight had filled me with so much rage that, had she not just died, I might have been tempted to use the blade on him. But I knew that she had intentionally given me the blade *before* Quetz could use it... And... As much as it pained me, I felt morally compelled to respect her wishes. Or her plan. Whatever it was, if she had one. I could only hope. Considering she was the other half of my soul.

Nuala was still asleep, recovering, slowly but surely, as the curse lifted and her body recovered from its death grip. She was going to be absolutely furious when she woke up and I wouldn't be even remotely surprised if she tried to murder us all for letting Aurelia die for her. But that was something I would have to deal with later.

I knew Caelus was coming. And now I was ready.

TWENTY-SIX

QUETZACOATL

"*For fuck's sake.*"

The words clawed their way out from my clenched teeth as I stared down into the inky black Waters of Kismet.

This wasn't supposed to happen. I was supposed to have gone with her. I'd scoured every single moment of the one potentiality in space-time that showed me Aurelia would survive another death and return to her body here in Aeternia...

But within that potentiality, I hadn't had that hysterical outburst. Kyril had decided to open his deranged mouth and asked those *ridiculous* questions. Wholly delusional in his confidence that he could actually find his way back here simply because he was her nexus mate. Or that we could just *pop open the doorway between realms for a second* so that we could let her back in.

If I wasn't so fucking devasted, I'd have burst into laughter again like a lunatic. Morwen had pried me off of Aurelia so she could enchant her corporeal body from decaying and had hidden it somewhere lest any other rebel fae, or Caelus, or Kyril, or anyone else get any dim-witted ideas about trying to do something to her. And even I didn't know where she was.

I'd tried what felt like a thousand times to scry and traverse space-time to find her for some reason. But I couldn't. It was like she'd disappeared from all existence. And it only served to further torture me. And without The Blade of Charon, that could only be summoned by those bound to it, the only way for me to die with her was to destroy my corporeal body. Which meant that I wouldn't be able to return to Aeternia with Aurelia, as anything other than some 'godly' version of a mute. That reality alone was the only thing that made me hesitate doing it.

But it wasn't a non-option.

I couldn't help recall Kyril's words...

"If I have to become a monster to protect you, Aurelia, so be it."

A deep stab of pained empathy bled within me at the thought. I'd literally be doing exactly what he'd promised if that's what I had to resort to... And... It didn't scare me nearly as much as it should have.

But first, I would pay a visit to the Waters of Kismet to see if there was another way.

EPILOGUE

AURELIA

A tingling lightness filled my body as my eyes slipped shut and the sound of Quetz's cries faded into the distance and only darkness remained.

Not in a bad way... Just... Different. I could still feel him. His spirit.

My own spirit seemed to lift, ascending like a piece of dandelion fluff on a powerful wind drawing it into the great unknown- the future.

Although the word 'future' seemed odd here. As did any sense of time or self. What sense of self I still had seemed to slip through my fingers like grains of sand...

Sand.. A shudder worked through my being, though I didn't quite understand why.

Peace was quick to replace it.

And this overwhelming sense of love. My entire being became consumed by it until it overflowed and spilled throughout all the infinite verses like some great permeating blanket of multiple dimensions, and all that remained was it. There was no 'I', or 'you', our 'we'...

There only was only 'being' and the infinite love that it held.

I could feel fragments, both one and many at the same time, of this being dying and being rebirthed... All at the same time. I could feel whole universes, worlds, distant stars and galaxies, and countless beings all dying and being reborn in violent unison.

It was a dark and simultaneously blindingly effervescent eternal force of life and death.

And binding it all was a sense of 'one-ness' and love.

I drifted like this for some... indeterminable amount of time...

Time, if it could be called such a thing.

Until, as though destiny had called and my spirit answered, I felt a part of my being drawn in a vaguely familiar direction. And I felt a certain familiar weight, and in response matter compressed, and a singular but seemingly separate consciousness returned. And water began to flow within me... Or no. Blood.

And I opened the eyes of a corporeal body.

GODDESS OF ORIGIN
SERIES BOOK 3 PREVIEW

THANK YOU

Thank you to my family and friends, who have been so unwaveringly supportive and believed in me even when I had a hard time mustering the strength to believe in myself.

Thank you to my readers. Words cannot even begin to express how grateful I am. The impact you have on the lives of my two boys and me is truly the stuff of dreams. I wish, from the depths of my heart and soul, that my writing has had at least a fraction of that positive impact on you.

Thank you to that source energy, guiding light, inspiration, the universe, the divine, God/Goddess, or whatever you wish to call it. I don't dare claim to 'know' what else is out there, simply that I feel there is something *so* much more beyond what we can even begin to comprehend or perceive. And that it begins and ends with love.

ABOUT THE AUTHOR

Originally from the US, Chiara Forestieri is a single mother of two [not-so] tiny little love muffins (a 17-year-old and a three-year-old, as of 2023) that spends her days taking care of her small family, practicing Brazilian Jiu-Jitsu and Muay Thai [with the grace of a failing inflatable tube man], pouring her heart and soul into creative and entrepreneurial endeavors, such as this book. All with varying degrees of success, of course. Ranging from 'well, at least no one died' to 'have you lost your mind?'

Currently, she lives in wonderful London praying desperately for sunshine and warm weather. And while many of her prayers have been answered, this one is most often not.

Some of her favourite things (outside of family and friends) include:

- Hot-warm-and-squishy freshly baked cookies
- Her Kindle
- Brazilian Jiu-jitsu
- Muay Thai
- All things nature and wilderness
- Animals
- Clean sheets (*drool*)
- Dirty humor
- The sea (her home)
- Sun

- Kindness
- Cuddles
- Oh, and love. Love, love, love. :)

Wanna see what all your favourite characters from The Goddess of Origin Series look like? Or see some of the most epic scenes from each book? Or just general juicy, steamy, romantasy content?

Follow the journey instagram! :)
@authorchiaraforestieri

Printed in Great Britain
by Amazon

17759061R00109